Dark Chapters: Daniel

Babylon

Hannah MacFarlane

© Hannah MacFarlane 2011
First published 2011
ISBN 978 1 84427 618 9

Scripture Union
207–209 Queensway, Bletchley, Milton Keynes, MK2 2EB
Email: info@scriptureunion.org.uk
Website: www.scriptureunion.org.uk

Scripture Union Australia
Locked Bag 2, Central Coast Business Centre, NSW 2252
Website: www.scriptureunion.org.au

Scripture Union USA
PO Box 987, Valley Forge, PA 19482
Website: www.scriptureunion.org

The right of Hannah MacFarlane to be identified as the author of this work has been asserted by her in accordance with the Copyright, Designs and Patents Act 1988.

British Library Cataloguing-in-Publication Data
A catalogue record of this book is available from the British Library.

Printed and bound in India by Nutech Print Services.

Cover design: Go Ballistic

Scripture Union is an international charity working with churches in more than 130 countries, providing resources to bring the good news of Jesus Christ to children, young people and families and to encourage them to develop spiritually through the Bible and prayer.

As well as our network of volunteers, staff and associates who run holidays, church-based events and school Christian groups, we produce a wide range of publications and support those who use our resources through training programmes.

Faith is being sure of what we hope for
and certain of what we do not see

For Anja, Charis and Becky

to ... ... or say He would be remembered for

Prologue

Etemenanki: House of the foundation of heaven on earth

They called him 'The rebel'.

He arrived after the flood that destroyed every living thing on the surface of the earth. Long after. But not so long as to have forgotten his great-grandfather's story or the instructions given to his family. The rebel remembered it all. He knew it by heart. It's just that he didn't really care.

The rebel was a strong man; a hunter and builder. Everyone who knew him admired and envied his strength and those who didn't had heard about it. The rebel was legendary and he knew it. He turned this knowledge to personal advantage. Though he despised them – the weak ones – scorned them for their neediness and easy compliance, he knew he could use them. And he would. The rebel would make himself indispensable. Little by little, he made the weak ones dependent on him, until they looked to him for everything and his tyranny became absolute. He laughed aloud to himself, thinking of what he would achieve because of his ability to control the people. He would be remembered on earth forever. But he wasn't satisfied. Being remembered wasn't enough. Not nearly enough. The rebel craved more than that.

He deserved absolute power.

'Your happiness is not God-given, you fools! Who told you that?' The rebel's plan was evolving. 'And you were stupid enough to believe it? No. It's because of your own courage – because of the work you have done with your own hands. What you achieve for yourself will make you happy. Only that – your achievements. Nothing else.'

The crowd hung on his words. They cheered at this revelation, only too happy to accept the lies he spoon-fed them. After all, he was the source of their lives' necessities and the one who guided their endeavours toward greater productivity and reward – a self-appointed leader among them – and they were grateful to have someone to think through the situation on their behalf. Both strong and intelligent, he was the obvious choice.

'God is not interested in you. Don't you fools remember that he almost wiped us out once before? Do you really believe he won't do it again? Really?' His eyes swept the crowd. 'We must take care of our own destiny. If God wants to send unending torrential rain to flood the land again, we will be ready.'

The people cheered again, their emotions roused by the morale-boosting speech and the dynamic of the crowd.

'I will build a tower. I will build it too high for the waters to reach, by my own skill, and with my own strength. I alone will ensure my future survival.' He watched the weak ones swallow it all. 'Which among you also see the futility of relying on God?' The rebel was enjoying this. They were nodding. 'Which of you have the courage to join me?' Another cheer. Louder and longer than before. He smiled. 'I'll look after you. I'll be your king.'

Sooner than anyone could have predicted, a tower rose high above the earth. Everyone needed and feared the rebel in equal measure. They had succumbed to both his logic and charm. According to his instructions they fashioned and burnt bricks, which they arranged in a massive square formation and joined with mortar made from bitumen. No amount of water would destroy the foundation of the tower he had conceived. It would not be permitted to enter or damage any part of it. With the rebel keeping a watchful eye on their exploits, the people were thorough in their work. Conscientious to the extreme, they were realising his vision at a phenomenal rate. The tower grew, layer by layer, higher and higher above the ground, with a staircase winding its way around the sides to its top in the heavens. It was a marvel of construction, an achievement never seen before. And around the tower, a city grew up. The rebel had drawn people together in one place and with one cause. To be their own saviours – controllers of their own destiny. He had revolted against the specific instructions of God. He had distracted the people from their true purpose, and prevented God's plan from being achieved. He was proud of himself.

But the rebel – Nimrod – would pay for his actions.

'Why have you stopped working?' Nimrod demanded. The building supervisor looked up. 'Speak to me! What's happening?' The man whispered with his friend but offered no response. Squinting sideways at Nimrod, he shrugged. He seemed uneasy. Nimrod was unused to delay. The audacity of the man riled him. He was incensed. Heat and fury exploded inside him and without warning he rammed his shoulder hard into the man's chest, knocking him to the ground. He kicked at his head until it bled. He would not stand for this insolence. He must make an example of this man so that the other weak ones would remember their place. They would respect him. They must. Suddenly, a group came at him from nowhere and started accusing him. They confronted him with angry voices and threatened him. He felt their anger, the force of their threat.

'Stop it! All of you, stop it now! You have no right—'

But he couldn't understand them, and they hadn't understood him either. He'd have to show the fools again. He grabbed one man by his shoulders, lifted him and threw him backwards so that he fell, folding awkwardly and screaming out in pain. Nimrod stormed away. He strode through the streets of his city, trying to regain control, but he was met everywhere with increasing confusion and chaos. Heated arguments reached boiling point and fierce fighting broke out between the workers. Every group opposed each other. He couldn't understand why they were all ignoring his instructions, his glorious plan to unite them and rescue them from themselves. He needed to rally them, discipline them, do something, but he couldn't decipher anything they said. His head spun. His knees weakened. All around him, he witnessed violence, segregation and fear. For the first time ever, Nimrod was afraid too. He didn't understand what was happening and this new sensation paralysed him with terror. His vision of common purpose was destroyed, but worse than that, he – the rebel – had lost the admiration of the people. They weren't behaving like weak ones any more. They'd found an inner strength and determination he'd never seen in them before. Control was slipping through his fingers like dust.

Nimrod had created a community. But it wasn't the one he'd envisaged, where everyone worked harmoniously with a common purpose to elevate their status – to surpass God. He'd created instead a city of utter confusion.

They called his tower 'Babel'.
The city became Babylon.

Part One

Jerusalem

I will remove Judah also from My sight,
as I have removed Israel.
And I will cast off Jerusalem,
this city which I have chosen,
and the temple of which I said,
'My name shall be there.'

Chapter One

I was born in Jerusalem in the reign of King Josiah.

While he rebuilt the neglected temple, I lay in my mother's arms. As he overthrew years of idolatry and false worship, I learnt to laugh and walk and talk. By the time he had put Yahweh back at the heart of Jerusalem, I was a boy, ready to listen and learn and emulate what I saw. I saw the legacy of a great man.

Those were the days that formed me.

That was my preparation for everything I would face.

Chapter Two

Babylon

Nebuchadrezzar hurried through the winter palace to answer his father's summons. He kept his head down as he walked across the courtyard but his hands and lips were animated, rehearsing their conversation. The furrowed brow and downturned lips on the prince's handsome face hinted at anger and passion, but his eyes softened it with sadness. At the corner, he turned through an archway and strode on through the maze of chambers. His steps were automatic, his mind elsewhere – engaged in preparation. As Nebuchadrezzar passed the throne room, his head turned involuntarily to look, but he knew he wouldn't find his father there. He glowered at the empty space.

This entire palace was all but empty. It was the middle of summer and the main palace was bustling. Nabopolassar had come here to escape that. He said it suited his condition better to be alone. He had brought only a few of the best to serve him. The winter palace, he had told his son, was a more fitting place. The unfinished sentiment hung heavily.

Easing into the room, Nebuchadrezzar took in his father's condition. Nabopolassar was pale. His eyes were closed. Even within the relative cool of the palace interior, it was warm, but layers of fabric covered his legs and body. An attendant touched the king of Babylon on the shoulder before drifting out of the room.

'O King, live forever,' whispered Nebuchadrezzar as his father's eyelids fluttered.

Nabopolassar's lips turned upwards. He opened his eyes a little and fixed them on his firstborn. His laugh was weak and gave way to a bout of coughing. Nebuchadrezzar stepped closer, knelt beside his father and took his hand.

'That is perhaps unlikely, but I thank you nevertheless.'

'Don't say that. You are a strong man. You will soon recover from this—'

'I brought you here to talk about the kingdom, Nebuchadrezzar.'

'Father?'

'I have taken Nineveh from the Assyrians—'

'A worthy victory. I was proud to be there with you.'

'—and when they fled to Harran, I captured that city too. Now they are settling on Carchemish as their new capital. They are making my Euphrates their home.'

'Don't worry about that now. You must concentrate on—'

With effort, Nabopolassar leaned forward and fixed Nebuchadrezzar's eyes with his own. Nebuchadrezzar swallowed.

'If the Assyrians are allowed to get comfortable, everything I have worked for during my reign will be worthless. Egypt has allied itself with them. The kingdom of Babylon must be consolidated now, while the advantage is still ours.' His voice cracked as he spoke. It was little more than a whisper.

'Your men will be waiting when your strength is back. Trust them to me. I will have them ready. Assyria won't present any challenge for you, even in a few months—'

'I can't wait, son. I can't afford to risk giving them time.' Nabopolassar coughed again. Tears formed in his eyes.

'Father, you mustn't think about this any more now. You need your strength for—'

'Go, Nebuchadrezzar. I want you to take my army. Finish this.'

Nebuchadrezzar's eyes were wide. He slowly shook his head. Nabopolassar laid back and let his eyelids fall. He whispered.

'O Nabu, defend my firstborn son.'

Chapter Three

Jerusalem

Four pairs of feet clattered through the Temple gate and broke into a run. Their duty fulfilled for another day, the boys were free. A couple of gloriously unplanned, uninterrupted hours stretched ahead of them and they planned to make the most of every minute.

'Come on!' Mishael was ahead of the rest and already impatient. His challenge was met – Hananiah, Daniel and Azariah sped up to join him. Tearing along the streets, jostling and laughing, the four boys raced. They were best of friends and fiercely competitive. They did not slow until they had reached the northern gate and the horizon stretched out lazily before them.

The four escaped to their olive grove. It was their favourite place to spend time together. Out of sight of their parents and the expectations of the adult world, they could relax.

'I'm being King Josiah today,' Azariah said with resolve, his eyes were fixed on Mishael – 'You were yesterday. You always are.'

Hananiah jumped in. 'Then I want to be Amon!'

Mishael nodded, already bored with the discussion. Hananiah smiled and sprang into position while Daniel settled back against an olive tree to watch.

'I am King Amon! I will worship the gods at the altars built by my father and you, my people, must do the same.' His proclamation echoed from the trees. 'Azariah, can you do this bit if Daniel's not? King Josiah's not in it yet anyway.'

Azariah approached the rock that represented the altar and attempted a chant. The boys laughed at the sound of his lone boyish voice in the fresh air. He grinned and instead made a performance of lighting a fire and bringing an offering.

'Come on, Daniel.' He shook his head. Azariah put his hands on his hips. 'You never join in with this bit. It's just a game.'

'No, I'm fine here.'

Mishael yanked on Daniel's arm to bring him to his feet. Hananiah joined in, grabbing the other arm. Daniel buckled his knees and kept his weight low. Despite his best efforts, his friends were stronger and pulled him up. He smiled.

'Don't spoil it,' Mishael said. 'You can pick your part. Whatever you want.'

Daniel didn't look away, but as his friends released their grip on him, he sat back down by the tree. 'I just don't like this game. Why do we have to think about Amon's barbaric policies anyway?'

'Because King Josiah wouldn't be the hero he is if he had nothing bad to argue against. He'd just be... boring.'

'Oh, please, Daniel!'

'Leave him,' said Mishael, watching Daniel. 'He really doesn't want to.'

Hananiah sighed as he returned to his role, but his enthusiasm for the pretence quickly returned. 'Your offering is pathetic!' he spat. 'Bring your son.'

Azariah rejoined the act, wrestling his imaginary offspring to the stone and binding him there with non-existent cords. He began the chant again. Daniel looked away.

'I won't sacrifice my firstborn!' Mishael piped up in mock defiance. 'And I won't worship your gods. Have you forgotten the lessons of your father?'

'You insult the gods and the king. For this, you must die!' Hananiah sprang at Mishael and knocked him to the ground. The two fought ferociously with olive branch swords, until King Amon slit the throat of his dissenter and Mishael groaned and flailed, hamming up his death scene. 'Your blood will flow through the streets as a warning to others!' Azariah gasped dramatically.

Hananiah went back to his altar, which was now a throne, and Mishael immediately sprang up. He grabbed Azariah and started whispering.

'What?' Hananiah demanded. 'What are you talking…?'

'We're doing the servant bit. Just sit in your palace.'

'Oh.' He sat on the rock and looked around. 'Did they really burn children?'

Daniel nodded. 'You ask me that same question every time. Don't you believe me?'

'Yes. It's just… It's grim. I don't understand why they…'

'And they had prostitutes at Solomon's temple.' It was Mishael.

'Prosti—?'

'Aren't you going to do the assassination?' Daniel interrupted. He glared at Mishael, who smirked and, eyes glinting with mischief, mouthed, 'What?'

Hananiah began to snore. The two conspirators crept up to him on tiptoe, one either side of the rock. Azariah grabbed his arms and pinned them behind his back. As Hananiah's eyes flew open, Mishael rested an olive branch across his throat.

'Help!' Mishael and Azariah smirked at the king. 'Not you! My own servants! I am betrayed by my servants.' He writhed to pull his wrists free. Mishael put a little pressure on his throat. 'Stop! I order you to stop. Would you defy your king?' Then his eyes pleaded with his tormentors and his voice trembled pathetically. 'Please don't hurt me.'

In answer, Mishael slit the throat of King Amon with one flick of his olive branch. Hananiah played Amon's death quietly but with expression, agony and fear in his eyes. His body slumped to the ground. But Azariah trampled the moment of pathos Hananiah had created before it had even registered with his small audience.

'What next?'

'It's your part,' Daniel reminded him. 'King Josiah.'

'Good. Shall we do the ceremony?'

'No, that's too dull,' Mishael decided. 'Go straight to the good part.'

'In that case, I'll need your taxes.' He opened his palm and waited. Mishael rolled his eyes. The others came forward and paid their dues to the newly crowned king. Daniel stood up and presented his tribute to King Josiah too.

'May God go with you, King Josiah.' He bowed.

Azariah nodded. He turned to Mishael.

'Take this money and repair the Temple. It has been neglected and must be restored to its original glory. No detail is to be overlooked. Find the finest craftsmen.'

The boys busied themselves setting up workshop areas between the olives, one carving wood, another chiselling stone and Daniel supervising the work. Azariah watched from his throne, growing increasingly bored. Daniel insisted on the highest quality, even in this imaginary realm, so Azariah had to wait. Mishael and

Hananiah were sent back time and again to adjust minor details until he was satisfied. As he waited and watched the patterns of light falling through the olive branches overhead, Azariah's thoughts wandered. He was hungry. At last, Daniel decided the time had come to bring the craftsmen to the Temple to install their handiwork.

This was the moment Mishael had been waiting for. He'd been playing along with Daniel until his opportunity arrived. He rushed to Azariah, waving his hands in the air, enjoying the mock excitement and the attention it brought him.

'King Josiah! A discovery has been made in the Temple.' Azariah, mouth stuffed full of olives, was jolted back to the game.

'Come,' he managed, still chewing. 'I will hear your news.'

'The Book of the Law has been found in the Temple of the Lord.'

He swallowed. 'What book?'

'The book has been unearthed during our construction work. It has probably been lying neglected for years. It concerns the Law of the Lord of Moses.'

'Thank you. I will have my servant read me this "Book of the Law".'

Mishael went back to his work on the Temple renovation, only to be interrupted after a few seconds by the wailing of King Josiah. Azariah was now pretending to tear his kingly robes. The other boys gathered around him, asking in concerned voices, 'What is it? What has upset the king?'

'Great is the Lord's anger that burns against us because…'

'… those who,' prompted Mishael.

'… those who have gone before us… have not obeyed the words of this book. No longer will we tolerate idols and impostors. The God of Moses—'

'Who brought us out of slavery…'

'Yes… will be worshipped in Jerusalem. And no other. Now go and find out about this God for me.' Azariah flung himself down, weeping and wailing.

Mishael ran two fast laps round the grove, grabbing hold of olive trunks to pivot around them without slowing, and returned to Azariah.

'I saw the prophetess, in the new quarter of Jerusalem. She says that God says…' Mishael inhaled, lowered his voice to a whisper and slowed his speech for effect. '"I am going to bring disaster on this place and its people, according to everything written in the book the king of Judah has read. Because they have forsaken me and burned incense to other gods and aroused my anger by all the idols their hands have made, my anger will burn against this place and will not be quenched."'

'Bring me the images of the gods. Bring me the statues and carvings and everything that has been used to worship them.' Then, in his most dramatic voice, Azariah added, 'I will destroy it all.' He considered adding a hollow laugh, but decided against it. He'd never heard the king behave that way.

The boys brought olive branches and clusters of the ripe fruits and piled them in front of Azariah. When they had collected a large pile, Azariah took one from the top and smashed it against a rock. The branch cracked and the fruits burst, sending juice spraying onto the ground around and flesh dribbling down the rock.

Mishael grabbed a handful of olives and hurled them against a tree. Azariah did the same and soon all four boys were laughing and squealing as they covered one another.

'Boys!'

They didn't want to find out who that voice belonged to. The four ran back to the northern gate, abandoning the throne of King Josiah and the shattered idols in the olive grove.

'Do you think King Josiah really destroyed all those things?' Azariah asked when they were at a safe distance.

'Probably not. But people like a good story, don't they?' Hananiah replied.

'It's not just a story,' Daniel said. 'My parents remember it all happening when we were small. Josiah rid Jerusalem of idols and altars to lots of other gods.

And he dug up the graves of priests who'd led the worship and burned their bones on their own altars.'

'You're making that up.'

'It's true. People were outraged about it. They thought he was denying them their rights.'

'All because of something he read in an old book?'

'Yes.'

'When I'm king, I'm going to be like Josiah,' Mishael announced. 'People really listen to him because he's not afraid of anyone. He just does what he likes.'

'He does what he thinks is best. And not everyone likes what he's done.'

Hananiah had been quiet until now. 'Do you think the rest of it is true? What the prophet said? That because people made idols and burned incense to other gods and ignored that book, God's anger will burn against us?'

'Yes.' The boys were quiet. Unusually thoughtful. 'And not be quenched.'

Chapter Four

Carchemish

Nebuchadrezzar's head hung low. He was doubled over, his chest heaving with each gasping breath. Sweat dripped from his forehead, ran through his matted hair and landed in the dust at his feet. Everything was blurred. He was consumed with exhaustion but his spirit was elated. It was over. The city on the Euphrates belonged to Babylon now – Carchemish was his – and Nebuchadrezzar was triumphant. As he allowed relief to sweep through his body, tension and strength giving way to heaviness and pain beginning to surface in his consciousness, Nebuchadrezzar's mind was buzzing. He doubted that anything could compare to this sensation of victory. His first. He must reward the men. He must get word to his father. He would order a building project to commemorate the occasion.

Nebuchadrezzar's knees buckled. He put a hand on the ground to steady himself. It was shaking. A barely audible rumbling came to Carchemish, carried on the Euphrates. He recognised it – it would swell to become thunderous.

He was in command of himself in an instant. He blinked, grimaced, and with a roar that began deep in his stomach and carried across the water, right hand grasping his sword, Nebuchadrezzar sprang up. The Egyptians had arrived. Before he was fully upright, he was running. His powerful legs pounded the earth. His arms pumped hard. With only the crown prince's actions for a command, his army mobilised themselves.

Nebuchadrezzar approached the first wave of Egyptian soldiers. They were intimidating in a way Assyria could never have aspired to. Their chariots moved easily across the rough terrain and approached him like a sandstorm. The archers were braced on their platforms, bows drawn, ready to strike. The bronze arrow tips glinted. But Nebuchadrezzar's faith in the men who had served his father so well was unshakable. His privileged childhood in Babylon had not taught him failure or fear. He had confidence in himself, confidence in their combined years of battle experience and knew too that they were feeding on the adrenaline of recent success. He could feel their energy and hear their defiance. They would make him proud. He lifted his shield across his face and chest and charged at the Egyptians. Their bows would be useless at close range and he wouldn't give them time to snatch up their spears.

An arrow whistled over Nebuchadrezzar's head as he sprinted between two black mares. For an instant, there was only the violent pounding of their hooves and a blur of darkness. Then came the dizzying motion of spokes in the chariot wheels. He hauled his shield above his head momentarily until the rising dust whispered that he had broken through. The threat from the charioteer's arrows was gone. Their focus remained ahead. Nebuchadrezzar left them to die at the hands of his men and did not look back.

A thick layer of choking dust swirled in the air around him, thrown up by the horses' hooves and chariot wheels, obscuring the scene like mist over the Euphrates, but Nebuchadrezzar ran on. He was heavy and muscular, but agile. Around him metal clashed, horses reared and men fell. He wove a deft path through the chaos. The stench of blood was obscenely pungent. Gasps of agony and the gurgling of death rang in his ears. These were indelible scenes, soul-destroying in their brutality, yet he remained focused. Bodies lay mutilated, twisted and crushed in the dust. Eyes stared, cold and vacuous. He pushed through. Engulfed in battle, Nebuchadrezzar was preoccupied, resolute. Only one thing mattered. One man.

Neco.

Nebuchadrezzar singled out the pharaoh to confront him. This was personal. The meeting of two great powers – ruler to ruler, man to man.

'You arrive too late.'

Neco halted his horse in front of Nebuchadrezzar. His solid position on the creature's back remained proud. His quiver of arrows was full, his sword ready. The young soldier faced him, breathing hard. Nebuchadrezzar's tunic was spattered in blood and exhaustion threatened to overwhelm him. His heart was pounding in his head. The sound of clashing swords rang in his ears. He ignored it all. The man in front of him was the reason he was here. Pharaoh Neco of Egypt. Defeating him would ensure his reputation and consolidate the extensive kingdom Nabopolassar had worked for years to build. Nebuchadrezzar was ready.

'We have taken Carchemish and obliterated Assyria.' Nebuchadrezzar was confident in his declaration. 'You are too late to help them.'

Neco laughed. 'The last man to oppose me died by my arrow. King Josiah attempted to deny my passage through Israel and returned to his Jerusalem a corpse. Do you invite the same treatment?'

Nebuchadrezzar stood his ground. His shoulders were back. Chest proud. Head high.

'Where is your father? I want to fight a man, not a child.'

'And I have no desire to fight a coward – but you sent your men ahead to greet me. Are you unfit to lead them or simply unwilling?'

Neco's eyes narrowed. His hand reached for an arrow. Nebuchadrezzar's reaction was faster. He seized his chance while Neco momentarily released his hold on the horse. His sword slid across the throat of the beautiful stallion in a single swift movement. The horse bucked, throwing Neco off balance. His bow plunged to the ground as he clutched at its mane. He clung desperately as the horse skittered and thrashed its head, its hind legs pawing at the ground, swiping through the air, and its body lurching violently in panic. Nebuchadrezzar fixed his eyes on Neco, instinctively dodging every writhing movement of the horse. Neco grasped for his sword, slipping, gripping, determined to regain control. His knees pressed in. His white knuckles strained to keep their hold. His eyes glowed with anger, but betrayed his fear. Nebuchadrezzar waited. His feet were planted, his knees braced, sword drawn. Looking Neco in the eye, he snarled. The horse reared. Its forelegs rose high into the air, eyes wide. The strong haunches gave way. Its legs descended to the ground and, using the last residue of strength, it bolted, galloping free of the horror, defying its great master, throwing Neco to the ground.

Nebuchadrezzar looked down. He positioned the tip of his sword at the back of Neco's neck. Neco scrambled to push himself up. He felt the cold metal touch his skin and his body slumped back to the dust.

He growled. Nebuchadrezzar kicked at his side to flip him over. Neco had no choice. He obliged. His face was lacerated and dirt stuck to his wounds. His hair was matted, his linen robe wet with sweat. Nebuchadrezzar had stripped him of all his Pharaonic dignity. His sword rested on Neco's throat.

'I will not die by your arrow today.' An image of Nabopolassar flashed into Nebuchadrezzar's mind. 'Today,' he paused, 'you will die by my sword.' This is what his father had sent him to do. This moment would secure Carchemish and it would be glorious. Nebuchadrezzar wrapped the fingers of both hands around the hilt of his bronze sword. He touched the notch of Neco's jugular with the point. His chest rose as he positioned his weight. He leaned forward. Neco shuddered. He didn't speak. His eyes were hard and cold. Nebuchadrezzar pushed down. He felt Neco's skin pierce. Felt the resistance of his flesh. He pushed. Listened to the air expelling itself from Neco's lungs. Pushed. Saw the blood creeping out from the metal blade and spilling along his clavicle. His sword touched the ground. He drew it back. The edge that had sliced through slid out smoothly. Blood pooled around Neco's half-severed head. Nebuchadrezzar was quiet and still. His focus was lost in the eerie whites of Neco's eyes and he didn't see the dark-haired man arriving on horseback. He heard the chaos as the Egyptians abandoned the fight and fled, but not the gentle footsteps approaching. He smelled the iron in the pool of blood at his feet, tasted his own sweat on his lips, but never had time to sense the thrill of victory that would have followed.

Nebuchadrezzar knew the messenger was there because the hair on his arms stood up.

Chapter Five

Jerusalem

Daniel, Mishael, Hananiah and Azariah stood at the gate of the Temple complex. They had come to lament Josiah on the fourth anniversary of his death, and make their offering to Yahweh. It was a long time since they'd played in the olive grove, celebrating the king who had been such a heroic figure in their young lives, and it felt even longer. Now they were young men with subdued spirits. In a few short years the character of the Jerusalem they had loved had altered. Josiah's son, Jehoahaz, had been selected to take the throne after his father's death, but had been captured and taken to Egypt almost immediately. Neco had instead installed his brother, naming him Jehoiakim, and imposed a heavy tribute of silver and gold, meaning that Jerusalem was no longer free. It operated as a vassal state, unsettling the population and ensuring poverty. Jehoiakim protected his own interests by taxing the citizens heavily, a policy for which he was deeply resented. When the news of Neco's death at Carchemish reached Jerusalem, King Jehoahaz was quick to transfer his allegiance to Nebuchadrezzar but that made little difference to his people. Resources that had once belonged to them still flowed out of Jerusalem, only now they went to Babylon instead of Egypt. Unrest gradually enveloped Jerusalem.

A raucous crowd at the gate was preventing the young men from entering the Temple. Another protest was under way. Daniel strained to see through the chaos to learn its cause, unable to hear anything except the jeering and shouting. Mishael was the first to get frustrated. Head down, he elbowed his way into the crowd and forced through to the front. His friends followed, buffeted and bruised by the jostling crowd, until a single voice surfaced above the rest.

'You have not listened to the prophets. They said, "Turn everyone from his evil way and from the evil of your deeds and dwell on the land which the Lord has given to you and your forefathers for ever and ever..."'

'Jeremiah's back,' Mishael informed his friends as they emerged from the mass of angry citizens behind him.

'I'm not surprised they're so furious then,' said Azariah. 'People hate him.'

Daniel watched the prophet with rapt attention.

'Daniel's not like most people,' Mishael quipped, gesturing towards their friend.

'No,' Azariah agreed with a smile. 'He's not.'

'"… Do not go after other gods to serve them and to worship them, and do not provoke me to anger with the work of your hands."'

Hananiah sighed. They'd heard this so many times, and yet carved figures and golden statues had found their way back into the Temple with inappropriate speed after Josiah's death. The thought of Yahweh's anger still terrified Hananiah as much as it had when he was a child. He didn't understand why nobody else cared. The evil that had haunted his childhood in stories had now returned to plague his reality. And he hated it.

'"I will send Nebuchadrezzar, King of Babylon, my servant, and will bring them against this land… this whole land will be a desolation and a horror."'

Mishael and Azariah were still chatting to one another.

'Shhh,' urged Hananiah, eyes wide and fearful. Azariah challenged him. The three began to argue. But Daniel was oblivious to his friends and the crowd behind him. He heard every one of Jeremiah's words.

'"These nations will serve the king of Babylon seventy years."'

Seventy years. Daniel internalised Yahweh's promise.

The Temple was filled with the heady scent of incense. Inside the walls of the Court of the People, strange inanimate figures stood on plinths. Flickering candlelight threw elongated shadows onto the walls amid a haze of smoke and distorted people's features as they prayed to gods of the sun. Every conceivable deity was represented. Every foreign god that Josiah had despised had returned to the temple that Solomon had built. Yahweh's Temple. These idols were lifeless. Powerless. Carved and sculpted by the same hands that now brought sacrifices before them.

Daniel could not get Jeremiah's words out of his head as he looked around the court. He burned with anger. *It's because of you,* he wanted to shout. *Because of you this city – our home – will be destroyed! Don't you remember that we were in bondage once before? We were slaves. Can't you see that it's going to happen again? We're going to lose everything. Our home. Our freedom. Our dignity. For what? For a temple full of glorified scarecrows! Yahweh brought us here. His power freed us. His power sustained us. Have you forgotten that? Can these gods help you now?* Daniel stood at the King's Gate and faced across the Court of the People to the gate that led to the Court of Priests and, beyond that, the Separate Place – the Holy Place, where Yahweh dwelt with his people. A place forgotten – ignored – by the people of Jerusalem. He knew that releasing his anger here would be worthless. Shouting and stamping and smashing the idols would have no effect on the people. Daniel restrained himself from unleashing his anger. It would achieve nothing except to make him unpopular. But he took a stand. Every other worshipper in the Temple faced the East Gate of the People's Court and beyond it the sun. Every worshipper was now confronted with a vision of Daniel.

Daniel alone faced Yahweh.

In the palace, the servants presented King Jehoiakim a scroll. An official had seized it from Jeremiah. On it was his prophecy. As the king read the words, his expression hardened. Every few lines, he ripped off a strip of writing, screwed it up and hurled it into his fire pit. The flames devoured the parchment, piece by piece, until the entire prophecy was destroyed.

Chapter Six

Babylon

'May the king live forever.'

'The king is dead.'

There was an awkward silence in the throne room as everyone turned to look at Nebuchadrezzar. The principle nobleman gestured for everyone to resume their conversations before drawing Nebuchadrezzar aside. He spoke quietly, but with sincerity in his voice.

'Nebuchadrezzar, you must understand... I am most sympathetic for your loss, of course... but this kingdom has been without a king for almost a month. The insecurity is growing—'

'At my father's request, I was in Carchemish, securing this kingdom. I came as soon as I received news.'

'I am aware of the distance you have travelled.' Nebuchadrezzar nodded. 'During your absence, I have pained myself to preserve the kingdom for your return. There are others who would have usurped you.'

'I am certain that you speak truth.'

'Then you must understand the importance of haste in this matter.'

Nebuchadrezzar stared. 'Haste? My father is dead! I will not simply seize everything that belonged to him the instant I return to Babylon!' He had raised his voice to a shout. Everyone present turned their attention to him again.

'It was his wish that you should inherit his dominion. All Mesopotamia will be under your command.'

'And what will I do with all Mesopotamia?' The veins in Nebuchadrezzar's temples pulsed. His eyes narrowed. The nobleman was unperturbed. He spoke calmly.

'Rule it wisely. I know you are capable. Your father knew it too.'

'Don't speak of my father!' Without warning, his hand flew up and slapped the nobleman hard across the cheek. The sound reverberated through the room. Nebuchadrezzar's eyes blazed. No one dared meet their challenge.

As Nebuchadrezzar's forearm descended to his side, a delicate hand slid onto it and rested there. The touch was familiar and quieted him. Though his face remained stormy, the anger drained away and his heart softened. Amytis stood silently at his side. She waited. When she felt the last of his tension leave his shoulders, she looked into his eyes and understood his fear. He understood his wife's unspoken guarantee of support. She kissed his forehead.

'Welcome home, great King of Babylon. Your victory over Neco is a good sign. Your reign will be long and prosperous.' He closed his eyes and exhaled. Tears formed and ran down his cheeks. Amytis wiped them away. He hung his head. Long moments passed. Noblemen waited, holding their breath, as the crown prince agonised. The silence was tense. But when he breathed in, Nebuchadrezzar inhaled all the status and dignity of his new position. The decision was made. His chest proud and head held high, Nebuchadrezzar opened his eyes a king.

As King Nebuchadrezzar positioned himself in front of the throne and waited for the principal nobility of Babylon to carry out the formalities, he whispered to his wife.

'Neco left me a gift.' Just as he hoped, Amytis' intrigued eyes posed the question he longed to answer. 'He installed a puppet in Jerusalem.'

Chapter Seven

Jerusalem

'Daniel!' Mishael skidded across the dusty ground and stopped by the wall where Daniel sat. Daniel looked up. 'Have you heard what he's done?'

Daniel smiled. 'What who's done?'

'Jehoiakim.' Mishael was frustrated. He propelled the name from his lips with distaste and kicked the wall.

'Slow down, Mishael. I haven't heard anything.'

As Mishael replied, he moved constantly, unable to contain the emotional energy flooding through him. 'The tribute. He's stopped it. Nebuchadrezzar failed a couple of minor campaigns somewhere so Jehoiakim's decided to send the gold to Egypt again.' Daniel exhaled. He was weighing the news. 'Hasn't he heard the prophecy? Is he completely stupid? Or just reckless?'

'Perhaps both. But he's still king.'

Mishael stomped back and forth in front of Daniel. 'Why can't that man lead? He's far more interested in himself than guiding the nation through this threat. It's always...'

'Mishael?' Daniel waited until his friend looked up. 'It may not make any difference. If Yahweh is going to destroy Jerusalem, he'll do it. With or without King Jehoiakim's help.'

Nebuchadrezzar's army marched through the outlying villages and farmland. They approached in battle formation, sending people screaming, terrified by the sight of their drawn swords. They cried out to warn one another. They grabbed each other and fled for their lives, but the wall of heavy, muscular men closed in. They were too close, and gaining ground. Farmers abandoned their tools. Mothers, terrified, scooped up their children. They sprinted to escape. The weakest died first; anyone who fell behind, stumbled or got separated. Babylon's men were merciless. They stabbed infants, sliced the throats of the elderly, slaughtered everyone in their path. Tears ran down the faces of the children. Piercing cries and agonised wailing filled the air. Nebuchadrezzar's men had the people surrounded. They were trapped. They had nowhere left to go. Shaking, sobbing and paralysed with fear, they clung to one another. They never reached the safety of the city walls. They died in the fields where they had worked. Their blood ran, polluting the ground, until it dried up. No one had seen the soldiers coming. Jehoiakim hadn't thought to send watchmen. The signal fires from the outlying garrison had been extinguished, but nobody had noticed. Babylon's army had arrived.

Famine came quickly to the city of Jerusalem. The crops in the outlying fields had been destroyed by the Babylonian soldiers who had now set up camp around the city walls. There was no chance of accessing anything that remained. The soldiers kept the food outside the walls and the mouths inside. The people of Jerusalem were trapped – besieged by their oppressors – and hope for survival was waning. Egypt had not responded to Jehoiakim's request for help.

As he watched his neighbours still clinging to their carved figures for comfort, Hananiah feared that Yahweh's anger would increase.

'Why am I being punished, Daniel? What have I done to anger Yahweh?'

'This won't last forever. The Babylonians will leave Jerusalem…'

'They're intent on destroying us!'

'… but not alone.'

The nobility suffered the lack of food alongside the workers. The storehouses were emptied and no one, not even the wealthiest, was spared the aching pangs that kept them awake at night or the weakness that threatened to overcome their bodies. Nothing could save them from the growing despair or the spreading plague. Either they would die in Jerusalem, from starvation or disease, or they would die at the hands of Nebuchadrezzar's men when he finally decided to attack. Who would have strength to defend the city? Who could protect their families now? The citizens doubted their king's ability to resolve the situation. In their desperation, they even began to doubt one another. Jeremiah continued to prophesy and advise, but his words were received with more derision and resentment than ever. And then Jehoiakim died and everything changed.

Nebuchadrezzar walked with his chief officer. The siege was progressing nicely and he'd come to assess the situation before deciding on his next move. Their journey around the city walls was leisurely. He had the upper hand and there was no need to rush matters. The king stopped at the foot of one of the siege ramps to examine it more closely. His men had done a good job. They had quickly built up what was just a mound of earth from the top of the hill on which Jerusalem stood to the top of the city wall, but the ramp was secure and fit for purpose. The construction was solid. Nebuchadrezzar sauntered up a little way, kicking at the ground. It was compact. Dust rose from the king's heels, but nothing more substantial gave way. When the time came, his men would charge out from the mobile siege towers, along the flattened top surface of the ramp to breach the wall. They would be inside Jerusalem with the speed and ferocity of a whirlwind. Nebuchadrezzar was pleased.

'And the battering rams?'

'Already in place. We have one located either side of the gate. There are further rams in strategic places around the city walls if we need them.'

'Then we are almost ready.'

'Our spies report that a boy has been chosen to replace the king. Jeconiah, Jehoiakim's son. He's only a child.'

Nebuchadrezzar chuckled. 'Even better.'

Azariah was close to the wall when the first impact hit. The sound was deep and loud and he felt it in his stomach. The wall shook, the sound reverberating through the ground underfoot. Azariah froze. Terror gripped him. His mind stopped. When the second impact came, chaos erupted around him. People darted this way and that, unsure where to go or what to do, dropping their wares onto the street, scanning the scene for family members, calling and instructing one another. Azariah watched them. *This is it*, he thought. The third impact struck and a strange calm settled on him. There was no point panicking, he decided. Nebuchadrezzar was coming – he couldn't change that. And once inside the walls, Nebuchadrezzar would be in control. At that point, all this frenzy would count for nothing. Another strike to the gate, a crack, and Azariah walked calmly in the direction of the Temple. He had no doubt that's where the others would go. He would meet them there. As he walked, the first wave of Babylonian soldiers appeared out of nowhere on the wall, casting ominous shadows down on the ground. People shook with terror, eyes wide, screaming, pointing. Beside him, a woman collapsed. Azariah did not look back. As he turned a corner and the Temple gate came into view, Azariah heard the gate splinter and break under the power and momentum of the battering ram. The soldiers were in. It had begun.

Chapter Eight

Jerusalem

Mishael was not heading for the Temple. He knew that's where the others would be, and he considered going to meet them, but the lure of the action was too exciting. He headed towards the gate and slid into the doorway of an abandoned house close by. Flies swarmed around a shape slumped in the corner of the room. A famine corpse. Mishael turned his back and watched the action outside.

Babylonian soldiers poured in through the hole in the gate. They were focused, determined, intent on their purpose. Each man immediately took up his position in formation. Jerusalem's citizens ran, fleeing in the other direction, but Mishael stayed where he was. He was riveted, grinning, enjoying every moment of the drama. And things soon got even better.

The soldiers were making a commotion; their sandalled feet thudded on the street surface as they ran, there was the sinister sound of swords sliding from sheaths, gruff voices barked orders, intimidating the people of Jerusalem. In the distance there was a rhythmic tap, tap, tap. *The sound of marching feet on the street?* A procession was in progress. *Was Jerusalem presenting a counter-attack? Had Jeconiah organised an army? Had the people themselves risen up to resist Babylon?* Mishael's heart ached. He was torn. He longed to see where the sound was coming from, but he didn't dare risk moving any closer to the Babylonian soldiers. He stayed where he was, shuddering with anticipation. Should he just run for it? He was inclined to, unused to being the passive bystander. Mishael agonised over the best course of action, driven crazy by the enforced stillness. He didn't have to wait long.

The Babylonian soldiers stood their ground inside the walls of Jerusalem. Standing in formation in front of the gate, they were ready to advance into the city. But they didn't move. They'd heard the approaching sound. The commanding officer grinned. He wasn't afraid of anything Jerusalem could confront him with. He could simply continue in spite of the interruption if he chose, crushing it underfoot as he tore through the city with his men, but he preferred not to. He would let them come, let them walk straight into his trap. He waited, letting them bring themselves ever closer to the inevitable. It was more poignant. Sweeter. The procession drew closer and Mishael saw palace officials, servants of the king, guards and city officials. And at the centre, among them, walked the king of Jerusalem. The child. The boy who'd inherited the city at a time of siege, disillusionment and depression – who'd been handed a diplomatic nightmare

– had taken the advice of the prophets and chosen, rather than to fight, oppose and die, to surrender to Nebuchadrezzar and keep his life. In front of the soldiers of Babylon, the procession drew to a halt. The officials, guards and servants drew aside, creating a path for the king. Jeconiah walked forward. Despite his youth and inexperience, he was dignified in his surrender – he held his head high. He didn't speak. There was no need. Jeconiah's intention was as plain to the army of Babylon as it was to Mishael, who watched the scene. Babylon's commanding officer scowled and shoved his sword back into its sheath. He was put out. He'd been denied his display of might. He allowed Jeconiah to approach but shook his head in derision.

A messenger was dispatched as armed soldiers closed in around Jeconiah. The soldiers surrounded Jerusalem's king, isolating him from those in his procession. The young king looked round. He met the eyes of every soldier. And then he waited.

Nebuchadrezzar arrived to oversee the process. His only form of questioning was to narrow his eyes at Jeconiah, who simply nodded in reply. No words were spoken. Babylon's soldiers bound the young king, flanked him on either side, and led him away.

After Jeconiah was taken from the city, the real work began. It was customary in Mesopotamia to cream off the best the defeated society had to offer, taking them home and incorporating their skills. Nebuchadrezzar intended to do exactly that. His soldiers began the process of identifying those with something to offer Babylon. First nobility; those with money and education, those who understood the workings of society and who held sway at court. After them came skilled craftsmen; carpenters, artists, sculptors and metal workers, and then the men of valour, captains and trained fighters. The process was long. Ten thousand would be taken. While his soldiers questioned, shepherded, separated and listed the citizens, Nebuchadrezzar had his own job to do. He was searching the best of them for one man – the man who could be trusted. A man who could lead, and yet defer, who would do what he was asked, serve unquestioningly and who would remain loyal. Nebuchadrezzar scoured the nobility of Jerusalem. He examined each man, narrowing his eyes to peer into their souls. He prided himself on his excellent judgement of character. He knew exactly what he needed and he was confident that someone here would fit his requirements. One man did. One man who Nebuchadrezzar named Zedekiah and installed on the throne of Jerusalem, a nominal king. His puppet.

Mishael was dragged from his hiding place and questioned. They soon chose him to go. Mishael was relieved to find that Daniel, Azariah and Hananiah were also among those chosen to be taken to Babylon for what they could offer the civilisation. They were the sons of nobility. They could be moulded, shaped, taught the ways of the Babylonians. They could bring a fresh perspective, a new way of looking at things, and prevent Babylon from stagnating. More importantly, their knowledge base was removed from Jerusalem. Many were left behind, but not those with the capacity for free thought. Workers in the fields, labourers. It did not serve Nebuchadrezzar's purposes to leave Jerusalem completely unpopulated. Jerusalem could provide resources for Babylon. Zedekiah would be there to oversee the workers and ensure continued loyalty to Nebuchadrezzar. The weak were left, and anyone with influence or intellect to rebel against the Babylonians, to lead rebellion, was removed. They would remain under the watchful eye of Nebuchadrezzar's army in Babylon.

Nebuchadrezzar took everything of value. The temples were sacked. Treasures were looted. Jerusalem's time as a city in its own right was at an end. The city of Yahweh – the fulfilment of his promise – was now no more than an empty shell whose sole purpose was to supply the demands of Babylon.

Chapter Nine

They changed my name, but not my heart.

I was not as impressionable as Nebuchadrezzar believed. He chose me and my friends for our capacity to learn. He took us away from what we knew and taught us Babylon's ways and expected that we would change. We were young men and he planned to shape us for his service. He put us through three years of training in the language and literature of his people. We were exposed to the city – its culture and its gods – immersed in all it had to offer. Then we were deemed ready.

I became Belteshazzar – 'Prince of Bel'. I accepted the label, but not Bel, or Marduk, or any of the others. Inside I was always Daniel. I never forgot the name of my childhood, though I rarely heard it again. My God had written its truth into my soul and nobody could take it away. Not even Nebuchadrezzar.

He underestimated Yahweh. They all did.

Part Two

Nebuchadrezzar's Babylon

'How can we sing the Lord's song
In a foreign land?
If I forget you, O Jerusalem,
May my right hand forget her skill.
May my tongue cling to the roof of my mouth
If I do not remember you,
If I do not exalt Jerusalem
Above my chief joy.'

Chapter Ten

Babylon was like nothing I had ever seen. The city announced itself, rising up from the landscape, long before we arrived. It was an impressive fortress, a marvel of construction, proclaiming the wealth and power and talent that resided within. Aware of their own greatness, Babylon's walls seemed to gloat. Arrogance spilled out from within the city and washed across the plains, making me uneasy.

I took my first faltering steps along the processional way with a cramping sickness in my stomach and an oppressive ache inside my head. Disturbing images ran along the wall beside me. A bull leapt down from the surface, teeth bared towards me, and I recoiled. The vision, though I knew it had been crafted by hand, seemed alive. My heartbeat quickened as the masterful artistry wreaked havoc in my mind. No carving or etching I'd ever seen compared to this illusion – the proportions were real, the colour vivid. I stepped closer and stretched out a tentative hand to meet its cold surface. My fingers traced the smooth curves of the bull's sculpted, muscular form that protruded from the flat surface of the wall. I looked into the eyes of the creature and pulled my hand away. I was on edge near it. I turned my head away.

The opulent Ishtar gate loomed ahead. What struck me most was the colour. Bright, brilliant blue. Offset with regular rows of golden dragons, it had depth, vitality and brilliance. But looking at it, I felt hollow. I couldn't shift the nagging perception that this extravagance was a facade. The illusion was carefully and skilfully constructed, designed to allure, attract, captivate – yet void of real substance.

Inside the immense walls, only one structure – a tower – commanded my attention. It was a feat of construction that, even incomplete as it clearly was, defied possibility. Another statement piece, but what was it proclaiming? A pain pierced me behind my eyes. My hands pressed my temples to counter the pressure. Lies. I knew in that moment that's what the towering, multi-level ziggurat had been founded on. Lies. I was convinced. Led along the ceremonial street to Nebuchadrezzar's palace, I couldn't forget the discomfort of that comprehension, or dislodge the image of the tower from my mind. I caught only glimpses of Babylon's landmarks. Even so, I couldn't fail to notice the lavish quality of everything I passed.

Everything in Babylon demanded a superlative.

Nebuchadrezzar was no exception.

Chapter Eleven

Babylon

The citizens of Babylon lined the processional way to witness the return of their men. News of Nebuchadrezzar's successful campaign against Jerusalem had reached the city days earlier and the celebration was already under way. Nebuchadrezzar had given his people yet another reason to appreciate and admire him. Now, they were dizzy with anticipation of the return of their victorious soldiers, who would bring the latest wave of captives and spoils from the siege. The familiar excitement of formal state occasions and religious festivals flooded the atmosphere in the centre of the city, where people waited in the courtyards of Marduk's temple and around the base of Etemenanki. Residents chatted happily to one another while their children danced and played to the music that floated through the air. Work was on hold. Nobody thought of such trivialities today. Today, the army would return under royal command. Flags would fly. Babylon would welcome home its king.

Mishael, Hananiah, Azariah and Daniel were among the first in the procession after the highest ranking among the armed men. They were trophies of war. They passed between the enormous square towers of the Ishtar gate, open-mouthed at the brilliance of the tiles, incredulous at the height of its inner chambers and the thickness of its walls. Mishael stared at the relics on display. Hananiah and Azariah stepped cautiously over the bronze threshold, bemused by the use of such a decorative resource for this mundane purpose. But Daniel remained quiet. Marduk's dragons on the surface of the gate's towers had turned his stomach and he needed to prepare himself for anything else that might assault his senses.

A shout of triumph erupted at the first glimpse of the parade emerging from the gate. The sound travelled the entire length of the processional way, and continued swelling. Babylon's citizens applauded their success. They cheered and whistled and shrieked at the sight of their returning heroes.

Daniel's face remained neutral. He watched with interest, using this opportunity to observe the culture to which he must now adapt. He watched, listened, internalised. He wanted to remember this moment. He wanted his first impression of Babylon to last, because this was his only chance to observe it through unpolluted eyes. Daniel knew that he had to make Babylon his home for the next seven decades. To survive here, he would have to adapt. He recognised that time would change him; the culture of Babylon would gradually work its influence, whether he wanted it to or not. But Daniel didn't want to forget what Babylon represented to him as a young man arriving for the first time.

He mustn't let himself forget who he was.

Chapter Twelve

Babylon

Amytis ran to Nebuchadrezzar and smiled as he wrapped his arms around her. She rested her head against his chest. He kissed it.

'Your heart still beats.' Amytis looked up into her husband's eyes. Nebuchadrezzar laughed. 'Now I know you are home.'

'I am home.'

'Talk to me. Tell me about your campaign. You have been brave and led excellently and ensured the continued security of the kingdom, but...'

'But?'

She held his hand. 'How are you? Inside. Are you intact? You must have seen...'

'I won't speak of the horror.' Nebuchadrezzar pulled away from his wife.

Her expression remained hopeful. 'It will do your heart good. You can't keep it locked away.'

'Amytis, what I experience in battle – what I do for Babylon – is not for your ears.' He pulled his hand away.

'Don't shut me out.'

'You can't understand. No one who hasn't seen it for themselves can ever know...'

Amytis sighed. 'I want to understand. I could if you...'

Nebuchadrezzar was tired and his patience failed. 'I don't want you to! Don't you realise that? I don't want you to know what it is like. I do what I must do, I blind myself to the reality and focus only on my job just to survive each day! But when I come home...' He breathed. 'When I come home, to you, I leave those things behind. I leave my sword and I come to you, Amytis. And all I want to do is forget.'

'But you don't.' Amytis was containing her tears. 'You never forget. Every time you go, you change a little; you become a little more distant, a little colder. Your heart...'

'The celebrations are continuing outside. Why don't you go and join in?'

Amytis' lip quivered. 'I'd rather stay with you, Nebuchadrezzar.' She moved closer to him. 'I've missed...'

'I have work to do.' He moved away.

'Now? But...'

'I must welcome our new citizens. Officially.'

Amytis folded her arms across herself. 'You've brought more prisoners, haven't you? Nebuchadrezzar, you know how I... I can't believe...' Nebuchadrezzar was pacing.

'You know how it works, Amytis. If I leave the intelligent, the skilled and the charismatic behind, they will rise up and rebel. This way, I keep Jerusalem under control by removing that faction and leaving behind only the compliant, dependent poor, who will oblige us by providing our basic resources. And at the same time, I give Babylon a boost; new blood, new talents, new ideas to keep the civilisation blossoming.'

'Blossoming? The last thing I saw blossom was...'

'What?'

'Nothing. How many prisoners are there?'

Nebuchadrezzar stood still and faced his wife to answer her. 'Ten thousand will resettle here. A handful of them are worthy of training for my personal service. They'll receive the best I can offer.' He reached out to touch her shoulder. 'Please stop calling them prisoners. They're not. That couldn't be further from...'

'They're walled in on every side! They're taken away from everything they've known and forced to live in this place with all its strange ways and straight rivers—'

'Canals.'

'And look at stone and walk on stone, without a living thing in sight...'

'Amytis,' Nebuchadrezzar took his wife back into his arms. 'Calm down. They'll get used to it soon enough. I even have people to help them with the language so they can adapt faster. They'll get used to it.'

'Will they? Really?'

'You did.'

Amytis pulled herself free and ran from the room.

Chapter Thirteen

Babylon

Daniel and the other trophies were led to a large courtyard in front of a palace. The whole complex stood on a platform of burnt brick and was surrounded with massive walls. They had barely grasped its scale before they were drawn straight to its heart. Nebuchadrezzar had commanded an immediate audience with them in his throne room. Mishael went first, enjoying the exploration, the sense of adventure and wonder of this new world. Hananiah and Azariah followed, less sure of themselves and relieved to remain with their friends. They stood on limestone slabs, enveloped in walls of the same brilliant blue they'd seen on the gate as they arrived. Images of lions and palm trees greeted them here. Daniel considered their significance, wondering why Nebuchadrezzar had chosen them to appear here, in this place, the seat of his power.

Nebuchadrezzar entered and the young men bowed down. They were on his territory now, and at his mercy. When they stood, Nebuchadrezzar smiled. He took his seat on the throne.

'Welcome to my shining residence, the dwelling place of majesty.' He paused, giving weight to his words. 'You have been chosen.' Nobody spoke. They were on unfamiliar territory and uncertain of Nebuchadrezzar's meaning. He chuckled. 'You have much to offer Babylon. You are intelligent men, and strong characters. You look the part, too. I welcome such an addition to my civilisation. My Babylon is a place of culture, of great achievement and innovation. It thrives on learning. We have acquired and assimilated knowledge from all over Mesopotamia. We learn constantly from fresh, competent imports like you. You are as valuable to Babylon as the timber we trade from Assyria. And in return for what you do for us, Babylon will teach you. You will find our understanding far superior to anything you have experienced in Jerusalem. The river is larger – and filled with better quality fish.' He glanced fleetingly at Daniel. 'You will do well here.'

Daniel looked sideways at Mishael, expecting him to say something, but even Mishael was speechless.

'But this is to be your home now, so you must appear to belong. We'll start with your names. The rest will come in time.' He stood, examining the four, pausing in front of each, then swept out of the room leaving the friends perplexed.

Before they had chance to react, an official arrived. He didn't bother with pleasantries.

'You will enter the king's personal service, but before that is possible you will need to learn the Chaldean language and experience its literature. You will be educated for three years, during which time the king has seen fit to appoint you a daily ration from his table – the choicest food – and of his wine.

'Meshach,' he barked at Mishael. Mishael's shoulders tensed and he opened his mouth to speak, but the official cut him off, addressing Hananiah next: 'And you are now Shadrach. Azariah... the name Abednego will serve you here.' He thought for a moment and, with a curt nod to Daniel, pronounced, 'Belteshazzar.'

Daniel found his courage. 'How should we address you?'

'I am Ashpenaz. I am chief over all the officials who serve in this palace. You are my responsibility and it will reflect badly on me if you do not live up to the king's standards. You will have noticed that his standards are high. Keep them. Because I intend to keep my life.'

Chapter Fourteen

Babylon

Daniel couldn't sleep. The celebrations had continued late into the night, and he had a lot on his mind. He sat outside, breathing the fresh night air and looking at the stars above the highest layer of Etemenanki. In the stillness and silence, he could understand why the Babylonians believed it was a gateway to heaven. It certainly appeared that way now. Daniel breathed deeply and allowed himself to relax. He was grateful to have found a place to think; to unravel all his new experiences, and listen to his heart.

Yahweh, my God, he spoke into the air, *you've brought me here. Here. To Babylon. This city of... wealth and power and... conceit. You gave Jerusalem to your people, but – because of their stupidity – you have taken it away from us. Yahweh, I heard Jeremiah. I know you have given us over to Nebuchadrezzar for 70 years. Seventy years! That's longer than you left Israel wandering in the wilderness without a home. That's a... I'm young. Much of my life will be lived in Babylon. But everything is new and uncomfortable and... I don't belong. I don't belong here! I feel separate and different and strange and...* He sighed, staring at the distant stars in the vast sky, feeling insignificant. *I have been chosen for the king's personal service. I can learn the language. I will. I can adapt to the customs. I'll have to. But how can I serve Nebuchadrezzar? How? How can I look him in the face and obey his orders and listen to him praising Marduk, his god of 50 names? Yahweh, help me. I need your help. Don't let this place wear me down. Don't let its opulence entice me or its stories blind me to you. Speak above the noise and the confusion so I can hear you.*

Daniel looked around. He looked at the ships anchored in the Euphrates, the mud-brick houses, the palace, the temple, the walls and courtyards, the streets. *I don't want Babylon to change me. Let me change Nebuchadrezzar.*

Daniel felt calmer. He watched the sky lighten and the stars fade. He felt the warmth of the morning and heard the first stirrings of the city. He walked along the bank of the Euphrates and watched the huge iron gate open in the water where the river entered the city walls, allowing the first trade of the day to begin. He saw the brick makers fire up their furnace, stoking it to generate enough heat to begin their work. He saw the citizens for the first time as people with families and stories, strengths and concerns – not collective Babylonians – and decided what he would do.

'Ashpenaz?' Daniel began as he entered the room.

'It is still early. You are keen, Belteshazzar. This is good.'

'Ashpenaz, I cannot eat food from the king's table.' His words tumbled out faster than he'd intended. 'I know that it has first been offered to the gods of Babylon, whom I cannot serve. I will serve Nebuchadrezzar, but I cannot defile myself with his sacrifices. These gods are not my God.'

Ashpenaz grabbed Daniel's elbow and drew him into the doorway, where the thick walls would mute his voice. 'Daniel, I understand your difficulty. But you are going to have to leave your conscience behind if you hope to survive here. Nebuchadrezzar has appointed your food and drink.' He looked around to make sure they were alone. 'I am afraid of him, Daniel. If he sees your face looking more haggard than others your age, I will forfeit my head to the king. I've seen it happen too many times – to people who were friends.' He swallowed hard. 'I'm sorry, Daniel. I can't help you.' They stepped back into the room. 'Belteshazzar, you will eat the food the king has appointed for you. It is appointed for your good health, so that you may excel in all your endeavours. We will discuss this no longer.' Ashpenaz shrugged his shoulders and gave Daniel an apologetic look as he left the room.

Chapter Fifteen

Babylon

Amytis watched. She sat on a chair by the bed with her feet tucked under her and a blanket thrown round her shoulders to keep warm. She was concentrating on the problem of what to do. She watched her husband. She longed to help him, but the king wouldn't let himself be helped. Amytis knew there were battles raging, not just throughout Mesopotamia for control of the kingdom, but also deep inside Nebuchadrezzar. He was a strong man who didn't like to admit weakness. Not even the small imperfections. Not even to her.

Nebuchadrezzar rolled over with a stream of mumbling that Amytis didn't hear. She strained to pick up the words, even a few that might give her a clue to what was troubling him, but it was futile. Nebuchadrezzar was deep in sleep and slurred the words together like a mist blurred the boats on the Euphrates. He'd been muttering in his sleep for hours, his brow creased and his body turning this way and that, as if trying to shake off a bad dream. Amytis had tried waking him. She'd put a hand on his shoulder and spoken gentle words, she'd stroked the side of his face, she'd repeated his name, over and over. She'd been afraid to do more. She didn't want to jolt him back to reality too suddenly. Whatever had caused it, Nebuchadrezzar's dream had a tight grip on him.

Amytis hated what the pressure was doing to her husband. There were high expectations of the king of Babylon, and he had even higher expectations of himself. Nebuchadrezzar had always had absolute admiration for his father and strove hard to emulate Nabopolassar's success; his strength of character, his wisdom and decisiveness and courage. Nebuchadrezzar was determined to achieve even more – to see the full realisation of his father's vision for Babylon. Amytis knew he missed him – she saw the glimpses of the ache in his heart that peeked out from behind the iron gates he kept locked across it to protect himself. She saw the frustration when he longed to consult his father about matters of the kingdom, and couldn't. She knew his grief had been suppressed. He'd not been able to allow it the space and time it needed with the overwhelming employment and responsibility of his new position bearing down.

This was when it all came out. At night. In the darkness and the quiet and solitude. It was becoming a frequent occurrence. Amytis was tired.

'Amytis?'

'I'm here.'

'You're awake again. Couldn't you sleep?'

'No…'

'I had a dream.'

'I know.' She sat beside him and wiped the sweat from his forehead with the corner of her blanket. 'Was it the siege? Did you dream you were…'

'No. It wasn't that.'

'Are you worried about something? I know the daily decisions and responsibilities weigh down on you. You're tired. You need a break.'

Nebuchadrezzar kissed his wife. 'This was different. It wasn't the day to day issues. It was something bigger. I don't know what it meant.'

'It probably didn't mean anything. It's just your mind sorting out…'

'It meant something. I just… I don't understand what.'

'We should get out of the city for a while. You could leave someone in charge. We could take a couple of weeks and go into the country and you'd have time to relax and think and…'

'The bridge is half-built. There's a lot still to do with the Etemenanki project and I… I have something else in mind to begin. It's not a good time.'

'It's never a good time. You must make space for…'

'No.'

'Please. For me. It's important to balance your responsibilities with time for yourself. Your father would have...'

'Don't mention my father!'

'I'm sorry, Nebuchadrezzar. I...'

'I don't want to be angry. Not with you. I don't want to hurt you, Amytis.'

'Then think about what I said. You'll feel so much better after...'

'Stop! Don't push me. I can't just abandon everything. I have responsibilities.'

'Yes. I know. But you also have a responsibility to me. And to yourself.'

Chapter Sixteen

Babylon

'I'm not going to eat it.' Mishael spat out his words.

'We going to have to to,' Azariah replied. 'Daniel tried, but...'

'I'll just refuse. They can't force it down my throat, can they?'

Hananiah looked pale. 'Mishael, you could be executed for defying Nebuchadrezzar. Think what you...'

'I'm not going to eat it! They can't prepare food properly here. They don't understand anything.'

Daniel had been listening. 'You won't have to. Just wait,' he insisted. Footsteps were approaching. He lowered his voice. 'Ashpenaz has to supervise every official in the palace. He's a busy man.' The sound was close. 'We're not that high on his list of priorities...' Daniel finished in a whisper. '... and he can't possibly be aware of everything.' The guard entered the room. He'd been appointed by Ashpenaz to manage the day to day care of the young men and their training. The guard addressed Daniel straight away.

'Ashpenaz says you have to eat this. I'm not allowed to give you anything else.' Azariah rolled his eyes. Mishael pushed himself up from the table.

'I know. And I understand that your position here is at stake,' Daniel reasoned. 'So, I'd like to suggest that you test us.' Mishael stood still. He watched Daniel closely. 'Give us vegetables and water – we'll be happy with nothing more than that – for ten days. After that you can decide whether the diet has any unwanted effect. You can compare us directly to the others our age who are eating the king's best food.' The guard considered. 'It's only ten days,' Daniel reminded him. 'After that, you can decide what is the best course.' He looked at Mishael. 'And we will respect your decision.'

The guard dithered. He looked at the ceiling and bit his lip. Then he looked hard at Daniel. 'I'm supposed to… All right,' he said. He sighed. 'But only for ten days.'

'My command is clear. If you don't do what I asked, you'll be torn limb from limb and your houses will be reduced to a rubbish heap!'

Nebuchadrezzar was not in the mood to accept any nonsense today. He had not slept well. He'd been unsettled and anxious since that stupid dream, and wanted to resolve the issue as a matter of urgency.

The wise men of Babylon – all the sorcerers, conjurers, magicians and Chaldeans – stood before their king. Everyone understood Nebuchadrezzar's insistence, recognising his tone and the expression on his face, but knew the impossibility of fulfilling his command. They were aware of their limitations and his request today went way beyond them. Nobody here had the ability to do it. No human did. Their only chance of surviving this was to reason their way out of the situation. The atmosphere in the throne room was tense.

'If you declare the dream and its interpretation, you will receive gifts and reward and great honour.' Nebuchadrezzar switched off his forced smile. 'So tell me what I dreamt and interpret it!'

An old, venerable Chaldean stepped forward. He had served Nabopolassar for years and had considerable authority among the servants. His voice was measured and calm. 'O King, live forever! Tell your servants the dream, and we will gladly interpret it for you.'

Nebuchadrezzar's patience was wearing thin. He had made himself clear but his servants were stalling.

'You are bargaining for time. You know the command is firm. Tell me the dream!'

The lions on the wall behind Nebuchadrezzar came into focus and bared their teeth at the Chaldean. He noticed, not for the first time, the ferocity of their expressions and the sharpness of those fangs. He stifled a shudder.

'There is no man on earth who could do this for the king. No ruler has ever asked anything like this of any wise person. It is exceptionally difficult. Only the gods could declare your dream. We are all mortals. I'm sorry.'

Nebuchadrezzar's expression was stormy. His forehead creased, his fists clenched at his sides and he bellowed.

'Destroy all Babylon's wise men!'

The old Chaldean dropped his head to his chest as the roar of the lion rang in his ears.

Chapter Seventeen

Babylon

'Show me your progress on the new project. Have you solved any of the issues we discussed at our last meeting?' Nebuchadrezzar quizzed the chief of his architects. They were kneeling in one of the palace courtyards, poring over plans which were spread out on the ground.

'The foundation of the building would need to be close to the river or to a canal, either here or perhaps here.' The architect marked the proposed sites with stones. 'Meaning that the baked brick would need a thorough coating of bitumen to protect it. This is nothing new. We have successfully used the technique at several sites in the city. We believe it will be possible to incorporate concealed reservoirs into the foundations from where the water would be drawn, in quadrangles.'

Nebuchadrezzar nodded his approval.

'The higher levels will consist of staggered platforms, for which we will use large stone slabs. We intend to cover these in layers of reed and thick tar, then baked brick, bonded with cement and finally lead. The stone will take the weight of the layers above, and the deep soil required for the roots of the trees, because of the square foundations below. Drainage, by way of internal channels, would be relatively straightforward.'

'And in terms of moving water to the higher levels?'

'I have several of my sharpest minds working on the matter at present. One or two possibilities are emerging, but nothing is certain as yet. I plan to begin tests on a small-scale screw mechanism within the next week or two.'

Nebuchadrezzar got to his feet. 'Treat it as a matter of urgency. If you do not resolve that question, there is no purpose in beginning construction of the external structure. It is of central importance. I want to avoid any unnecessary delay.'

'Of course.' The architect gathered the parchment and scrambled to his feet. They began walking.

'I want you to assign extra resources to it. Nothing in Babylon has priority over this.'

'I understand.'

'Nothing.' They continued in silence for a moment. Nebuchadrezzar was letting his architect feel the weight of importance he'd assigned to this. 'It must remain a matter of absolute discretion. Nobody must know anything of this project. Which means that construction of the bridge must continue at its current rate. And that the renovation of Etemenanki must not be interrupted.'

The architect looked up. 'I cannot see how that is possible. I will, of course, do my best. But with the best of the architects and engineers concentrating on this new development, the teams working on the bridge and the tower have nobody to inspire their enthusiasm or to keep them from deviation and distraction.'

'Promote the best within those teams to leadership. Impress on them the importance of keeping the others motivated. You may recruit as many as you need from the recent influx of Judean captives to the work of brick-making and assisting with the movement of resources. But keep this new project to your most trusted workers.'

'It is done.'

'I will expect a report tomorrow, as to progress on the water issue.'

'Of course. But, King Nebuchadrezzar, there is one more issue on which I would ask you to advise.' Nebuchadrezzar nodded. 'The furnaces are in constant use; they produce a steady supply of bricks throughout the day. If I recruit more to the work of brick-making, the piles of unbaked bricks will simply build up. The furnaces themselves limit our production and the rate at which we can build depends entirely on them. Our final output cannot increase.'

'Have at least two more furnaces constructed. In the meantime, heat them hotter, so that the baking process will occur faster.'

'Thank you.'

'Not a word.'

Chapter Eighteen

Babylon

Daniel, Mishael, Hananiah and Azariah stood with the other young trainees. The guard was observing them, deciding what to do. He knew he should follow Nebuchadrezzar's instructions. And logically, these men should be looking weaker. This was supposed to be a straightforward matter. He had planned to come here, see that their diet had not been sufficient to sustain them and make their bodies thrive, and end this nonsense. That's the only reason he'd agreed to the test in the first place – it had seemed that it would inevitably end in his favour. But now it wasn't clear at all. If anything, the four who'd asked for the test seemed fuller-faced, stronger and healthier. They glowed with vitality. Their eyes were bright. Their skin had colour. He was confused.

His thoughts were interrupted by the sound of running feet, pounding the ground and approaching fast. He turned to see several of the king's bodyguards charging toward him. The guard looked at Daniel. He needed to resolve this. Whatever was developing here was clearly more pressing. 'Fine. We'll continue your way. It certainly seems to be working. I find no fault with you.'

'Are these the men you are training to serve the king?' demanded the captain of the king's bodyguard.

'Yes.' The guard hesitated. He looked sideways at the young men. When he spoke, he fought to control the wobble in his voice. 'Why are you here, Arioch? Is there a problem with the training? Is the king unhappy with the way they are... being managed?' The guard's cheeks flushed a little. His fingers were curling and flexing involuntarily behind his back.

The captain stepped closer and glared at the guard. 'No.' He turned to face the men. 'But it won't be necessary for you to continue.'

'What do you...?'

'The king has ordered me to put them to death.'

Chapter Nineteen

Babylon

Daniel spoke up. He wanted to understand why the decision was so sudden and irrevocable. Was this the temper of a spoilt ruler, believing himself beyond reason and reproach, or had somebody caused the king genuine offence? Daniel didn't know enough to decide yet, but either way, it seemed an extreme course of action.

'Forgive me, but what has happened to cause the king to issue such an urgent decree?'

'King Nebuchadrezzar had a dream. He asked his wise counsel to interpret it for him, but he insisted they also tell him the substance of the dream. None could, so now he wants the whole profession eradicated. Including you.'

'Arioch, I would like an audience with Nebuchadrezzar.'

'Are you sure?'

Daniel nodded.

Arioch whistled.

'O King, live forever!'

'Belteshazzar, if you are here to change my mind, it is too late.'

'I come with a request.' Nebuchadrezzar looked incredulous, but saw that Daniel had more to say. He had heard report of Belteshazzar and knew that, in training, he excelled beyond his peers. Something in Daniel's manner – sincerity, perhaps – also told him that despite his youth, this man had the decency not to abuse his time. The king, intrigued, waited to hear Daniel. 'I will bring you the interpretation of your dream. But I will need time.'

'You will bring me the interpretation?' Nebuchadrezzar laughed. 'I have not told you the matter of my dream.'

'I know.'

Nebuchadrezzar laughed again. 'Those older and far more experienced than you tell me this is impossible.'

'I believe it is possible.'

Nebuchadrezzar's amusement faded. His curiosity was stirring. 'If you return, tomorrow, and do what my entire wise counsel cannot, I will reward you greatly, Belteshazzar.'

'Thank you.'

Nebuchadrezzar narrowed his eyes. 'But if you are wasting my time, know that I will have you torn limb from limb.'

'Daniel!' Mishael ran to meet him. 'Where have you been? We thought...'

'I was talking with the king.'

'Talking with Nebuchadrezzar? The king has ordered your death and you decided to pop in for a chat!' Mishael landed a playful punch on Daniel's chest. Then he held Daniel's shoulders and looked him in the eye. He used a tone that rarely passed his lips. It carried weight. 'Daniel. We really thought you weren't coming back. We thought he'd have your head, for certain.'

'He's not going to kill us... yet.'

Mishael stared. 'What do you mean, yet? What's going on, Daniel?'

'Pray for me. Entreat Yahweh for his compassion. Ask him to spare us from Nebuchadrezzar's wrath. The king of Babylon is full of anger. Even with all this wealth and influence, he's unsatisfied and he's looking for people to blame. Today it was his wise men. Tomorrow, who knows? It could be anyone.'

'This is dangerous territory, Daniel. I thought I was the brave one, but...'

'I want to show him a God with real power, Mishael. Marduk can't reveal his dream, or Ishtar, or Nabu, or Sin. None of them. But Yahweh can.'

'Are you sure you want to do this?'

'We're going to be in Babylon for a long time. I'm not going to spend it all just hoping to survive, counting the days until we can go back to Jerusalem. This is home now. I need to live my life.'

'You think we're going back?'

'Eventually.'

'Daniel? What if Yahweh doesn't spare us?'

'Just pray. And tell the others.'

Mishael watched Daniel walk away.

Daniel lay on his back in the courtyard of Etemenanki. The stars were bright. He considered the renovation of the tower – it had grown significantly in the short time he'd been resident here – and wondered why so many people were making so much effort for Marduk; a Babylonian version of the carvings people had worshipped in Jerusalem. However lavish and painstakingly decorated, Marduk was still a scarecrow; crafted by human hands, an empty representation of a powerless, invented god. He sighed at the futility and waste of it.

Yahweh, Nebuchadrezzar wants to kill us. He's angry. He says it's because his Chaldeans can't reveal his dream. He blames them for not meeting his expectations and so he wants to kill us all. Perhaps he thinks it will make the problem go away but I don't think it will. I think it was the dream. I think it unsettled him, and he doesn't know why, and he doesn't like the uncertainty. Yahweh, you sent that dream. You want to tell Nebuchadrezzar something. I know you want him to understand his dream as much as he longs to understand its meaning. Yahweh, all wisdom comes from you.

You give understanding to the intelligent. Tell me Nebuchadrezzar's dream so that I may explain it to him. I am working hard to learn their ways according to their training so that I may serve here. You've brought me to Babylon from Jerusalem and I know you plan to keep me here a long time. Let me use that time to help Nebuchadrezzar. Let me soften the heart of the king of Babylon by serving him so that the whole city may be influenced and changed. Mishael says I'm brave. I'm not brave. I'm not afraid of Nebuchadrezzar. But I think Nebuchadrezzar is afraid.

Chapter Twenty

Babylon

'Arioch!'

'Good morning, Belteshazzar. It's a beautiful day. You should make the most of it. It'll probably be your—'

'Don't kill anyone yet! I know what the king dreamt. Take me to him, and I will declare it.'

Arioch rolled his eyes. 'Come on.'

'May the king live forever! I have found a man among the exiles from Judah who can make the interpretation known to the king!' Daniel could tell from the expression on Arioch's face that he didn't believe it; he just thought it was a good joke.

'Are you able to make known to me the dream which I have seen and its interpretation?' Nebuchadrezzar peered at Daniel, half hopeful, half disbelieving that such a young man could have anything of value to bring to the king of Babylon.

'You have asked about a mystery that no wise man is able to declare to you, but there is a God in heaven who reveals mysteries, and he has made known to the king what will take place in the future. That is what you dreamt about. King Nebuchadrezzar, you were thinking about the future and God has revealed to you the mystery that will take place. God has revealed your dream to me for the sole purpose of interpreting it for you, so that you may understand the thoughts in your own mind.'

'In your dream you saw a statue. It was large, and extraordinarily magnificent. The statue's head was made of fine gold, its chest and arms of silver, and its stomach and thighs were bronze. Its legs were of iron and its feet a mix of iron and clay. As you watched, a stone was cut out without hands and struck the statue on its feet of iron and clay and crushed them. The iron, the clay, bronze, silver and gold were all crushed at the same time and became like chaff from the summer threshing floors, and they were carried away in the wind until no trace of them was found anywhere. The stone that had hit the statue grew into a mountain that filled the whole earth.'

Nobody spoke. Nebuchadrezzar sat on his throne, open-mouthed. Silence hung in the air. Arioch shuffled his feet. Daniel waited. Nebuchadrezzar continued to stare. Without warning, the king rose from his throne and threw himself face down on the floor in front of Daniel. Daniel took a step back. He shuffled.

'Belteshazzar.' Nebuchadrezzar hesitated, collecting his thoughts. 'Your God is, unquestionably, higher than all other gods.' He looked up at Daniel, as if looking for the words. 'He is a Bel, a lord, over kings – even a king as great as me. And I know he can reveal mysteries because you have been able to reveal this to me.'

Daniel waited. He didn't want to intrude on Nebuchadrezzar's thoughts, which were clearly still racing. He sensed there was more to come, but did not expect what he heard next. Nebuchadrezzar, still kneeling, pushed himself up.

'Belteshazzar, I am making you head over the province of Babylon and chief over all the wise counsel.'

'Thank you, King.' He held out a hand to help Nebuchadrezzar to his feet. 'I'm honoured to be asked to serve you.' Daniel weighed his words carefully before he spoke again. 'May I make a request?'

Chapter Twenty-one

Babylon

Nebuchadrezzar sat in the boat facing his wife. He had brought her to the Euphrates so that she could be the first to see the foundations of his bridge. Nebuchadrezzar was excited. When this was complete it would change everything. The two halves of the city would have easy access to one another by road. Soon resources wouldn't have to be loaded onto boats to cross the divide. This would speed up productivity considerably.

'Here. This is the first of the brick piers that will support the weight of the road. They bake the bricks for strength, and cover them in asphalt to protect them from the water. And the shape allows the water to flow around smoothly. There won't be turbulence disturbing the boats, or undermining the pier.'

'And is it safe? It will have to support the load of many people travelling across it.'

'The army drive their chariots, each drawn by four horses, along the raised walkways between the inner and outer city walls. Why should this be different?'

'And what if someone falls?'

'I trust my architects. The plan includes a wall.' He smiled. 'There will be a whole row of those piers across the width of the river, to support the bridge, with enough space in between for a boat to pass through easily. The road will rise high above the water so that even the largest trade ships can still pass through to anchor by the market.'

Amytis trailed her hand in the water, enjoying the sensation of the warm sun on her face and cold water on her fingers.

'It's clever,' she said. 'I can't imagine how it's going to look when it's finished. It makes my head hurt trying to understand, but you've thought of everything. I think it will help the people, make things easier for...'

'And more importantly, it will increase the efficiency of the city.'

Amytis pulled her fingertips from the water and sat upright. The sudden movement rocked the boat. 'Is that all you think about? Efficiency and production and profit?'

'Amytis,' Nebuchadrezzar replied, holding the sides of the boat, 'I'm in charge of Babylon. That's my job.'

'And who is in charge of the well-being of its citizens? Isn't that your job too?'

'I gave my people a celebration to remember when I returned. The festival is happening soon – they have places to live, great food to eat and awe-inspiring things to look at every day of their lives. They're proud to be part of my Babylon. They have employment. They feel valuable...' His raised eyebrow challenged Amytis to disagree. She chose not to argue this time, but Nebuchadrezzar felt uneasy. He suspected that his wife's constant concern for the people wasn't entirely unselfish. He knew it probably stemmed from dissatisfaction with her own existence in Babylon. He was somehow letting her down, and that made him feel helpless. Amytis' emotions confused him. He wasn't good at interpreting or acting on them. He resolved to complete his gift to her. That would prove he wasn't completely insensitive. It was a gargantuan gesture that couldn't fail to impress his wife. It would allay her fears and discharge his marital responsibility so that he could get back to concentrating on more important matters of the kingdom. He felt more at home with those concerns.

For now he'd just have to distract her. Even that wasn't easy because whatever he talked about seemed to bring her back to this. But there was one topic that might do it.

'Amytis, do you remember that dream?'

'Of course, I...'

'I know what it meant.' He had her attention. 'One of the young men in training told me – Belteshazzar.'

'One of the Judean captives?'

'He told me what none of my counsel could.'

'You're sure?'

'He didn't only tell me the meaning. He first told me the dream.'

'He must have heard it somewhere.'

'Impossible. I didn't tell anyone. Even you didn't know what it was about.' Amytis leant forward.

'So…?'

'I'd been thinking about the future. My father worked hard to establish this kingdom, and I'm doing everything in my power to build on that and make it last long after I'm gone… You know I want to leave a legacy that lasts forever. But I do sometimes wonder. My dream was about a statue. Daniel said that I was the head made from gold. That represents the Babylonian kingdom.'

'What does it mean?'

'Wait. There will be more kingdoms afterwards, but not as great, so the statue had parts made of silver, bronze, iron and clay further down, for those other kingdoms.'

'Which kingdoms?'

'I don't know. That's not really important, because none of them will be as significant as Babylon – Babylon is the only gold part – and I'm the head of it.

'And then there was something about a kingdom in heaven that would crush all the civilisations and be bigger than any of them and endure forever.

Belteshazzar said it was his God in heaven that revealed the dream to him. That he knew the mysteries of the future. And he said it was this God who gave me my power and strength to rule over everywhere that men dwell and birds fly and beasts...'

'But the kingdom of this God will destroy Babylon?'

'Yes.' Nebuchadrezzar and Amytis looked at each other. 'Do you believe it?'

'Belteshazzar told you your dream. You hadn't told anyone?'

'No one.'

'Then his God must be real. How else...'

'I've promoted him.'

'Belteshazzar?'

'His God says I'm the head of a golden civilisation. It's true. I am. I've promoted Belteshazzar and I'm commissioning a golden statue to celebrate.'

Chapter Twenty-two

Jerusalem

Nebuchadrezzar was furious. He found himself back outside the walls of Jerusalem, examining his army's handiwork again. Because of Zedekiah. The name insulted his lips. He would not speak it again. The traitor. This was a waste of his valuable time. Jerusalem had been under his control, providing a steady supply of food into Babylon. He thought he'd chosen a reliable vassal in Zedekiah, but too many years as 'head of state' had given the traitor ideas. He thought too much of himself. Construction of the monumental golden statue was under way in Babylon – designed to be a reminder of Nebuchadrezzar's greatness that nobody in all Mesopotamia could possibly ignore – and this man was undermining the exact concept on which it was being built. Nebuchadrezzar needed to put him back in his place.

Nebuchadrezzar's men had been camping outside Jerusalem long enough now to cause the famine in the city to have reached a critical state. He had ordered them to make life unbearable inside the walls and they had done exactly that. Nebuchadrezzar would show no mercy. He'd make an example of them throughout

Mesopotamia. He wouldn't even spare the city this time. He could manage without Jerusalem. Especially if it was going to cause him this much time and expense in return for its meagre tribute. The traitor would be spared, though. Death would be too easy an escape for his crime. Nebuchadrezzar had something else in mind.

'O King, live forever!' The messenger's shoulders were heaving with every short breath. 'Zedekiah and his sons have fled Jerusalem by another gate. The army gave immediate chase.'

'My chariot,' Nebuchadrezzar said. His face was expressionless.

Zedekiah and his sons were bound and surrounded. They had not travelled far from the city before they had been overtaken and captured by Nebuchadrezzar's men. The Babylonian army had strength and numbers. Zedekiah had neither. Nebuchadrezzar stepped down from his chariot and looked with scorn and contempt at the men he saw. He watched their horror as they listened to the screams from the city. Nebuchadrezzar's men had breached the walls and swarmed the city streets on horseback.

Nebuchadrezzar nodded to one of his men. The muscular soldier grabbed Zedekiah and hauled him to his feet. Zedekiah kicked and struggled and spat at the soldier. Saliva was strewn across his face. His temples protruded and his cheeks were flushed red. He cursed and shouted. He looked possessed. The soldier held him. He writhed and fought with no intention of surrendering, but the soldier resisted every attempt he made. Zedekiah's protest was pointless. He had defied the king of Babylon, and he would pay for his insolence. The younger of Zedekiah's sons was dragged to his feet by his hair by a second soldier. He squealed in pain. Zedekiah stopped fighting. He stared at his son. The soldier holding him pulled his arms tightly behind his back and locked them there with one arm. With the other hand he squeezed Zedekiah's jaw to prevent him turning his head.

'King?'

'Begin.'

A bronze sword caught the light and deflected it into the son's eyes. He squinted. The man approached him, keeping the light trained on his eyes. The son tried to turn his head away but his hair was being held and pain seared his scalp. Then the thin, cold edge of the sword touched his neck. His eyes widened in horror. He felt a drop of sweat trickle slowly from his temple, down his cheek, intensely aware of every moment of its journey. Adrenaline was coursing through him and his nerves were sharper than ever before. He hated the sensation. He wanted – needed – it to end. He was dizzy. Zedekiah's eyes were filled with anger and sadness. He could not look away from the horror – could not bring himself to shut his eyelids to block it out. That would be betrayal of the worst kind. His son was being tortured because of his actions, and Zedekiah must suffer every moment alongside him. The soldier drew the sword slowly, deliberately across the boy's throat. The scream turned first to an agonised cry, then to a haunting hollow bubbling of fluid. Zedekiah's tortured howl filled the eventual silence. He sank to his knees, tears mingling with the mucus that flowed from his nostrils over his lips and dribbled from his chin. His chest contracted. The ache was deep. He couldn't bear it. He was sure that he would die, but the agony lingered on. His sides ached from the heaving sobs. His head was pounding. But it wasn't over yet. They had his firstborn, his eldest boy. Zedekiah's chin shuddered. His body shook. His sorrowful eyes fixed on his son, who returned a look of hatred. Zedekiah let out another wail. His son despised him. He was going to die and Zedekiah was powerless to change the way he felt. What had he done?

'Spare him,' he begged. 'Don't touch him!'

Nobody was listening. The sword was drawn.

'Kill me instead. Let him go. He's innocent...'

The soldier placed its tip on the boy's stomach. 'Stop!' Zedekiah saw his son double up as the sword plunged deep into his gut. He watched, horrified, as his son's legs buckled. The soldier drew the sword upwards, opening his stomach, splitting his chest, severing his heart. He drew it up through his neck to his jawline, twisted it round in his throat and then withdrew it. The boy's eyes rolled back to show only white. Saliva hung in long strings from his lower lip, which hung lifeless and limp. Zedekiah looked down at the brilliant red pulp filling the space where his son's chest used to be. Blood spewed out in streams, pooling in the dust. Entrails hung, dragged downwards by their own weight, and fell to the ground in a soft squishing slump. The soldier pushed the head forwards, forcing the face down into the innards of its own body and smearing them around on the ground, then releasing the hair. Zedekiah threw himself to the ground and wept.

Chapter Twenty-three

Babylon

'I've been assigned the task of pumping water for the garden,' the Chaldean began.

'And what's your complaint?' Hananiah asked.

'It is hard physical work and the shift is too long. My hands are raw from turning the handle to drive the screw.' He thrust them towards Hananiah, revealing large, red welts along the base of his fingers, some of which were blistered and broken or pus-filled. 'The amount of water required to reach the upper levels is enormous and weighs heavily so that the handle resists my efforts. By the end of my work, I can hardy stand from the ache in my back.'

'None of the other workers complain.'

'They do. It's just... Nebuchadrezzar will tear us apart if any of the plants he's introduced die before... They're afraid. I was chosen to come to you with the matter, to represent them.'

'The work must be completed,' said Hananiah. 'The king has ordered it.' The Chaldean hung his head in response. 'You may however, reorganise the shifts so that they are shorter. You'll each need to work twice per day to compensate. It won't reduce your work, but by spreading it across the day, it may seem more palatable. Work it out together and report on the new system to me so that I may monitor its success.'

'Thank you.'

'Daniel!' Hananiah was relieved to see his friend. He'd hardly seen him at all since beginning his new role in the administration of Babylon. Though he shared the workload with Mishael and Azariah, the status and responsibility made him uncomfortable. 'How is your work in the palace? We hardly see you!'

'Nebuchadrezzar's made my life very comfortable since I interpreted that dream for him. He's given me all kinds of gifts.' He held his arms wide, demonstrating the new garment he wore. 'I'm trying to ignore it though. It's not important. I don't want to be bought by the king, or influenced by him. I need to keep listening to Yahweh.'

'Daniel. Nobody can change you.'

'If only that were true.' Daniel sat down next to Hananiah and lowered his voice. 'They can, Hananiah. I'm not immune to Babylon. No more than anybody. I have to keep making the right decisions, day after day... I'm susceptible to becoming Nebuchadrezzar's puppet in the same way as the rest of his "wise" counsel.'

'Don't say that. If I can't believe that you can do this, what hope is there for me? I'm not as strong as...'

'Yahweh. Be certain of your God, not of me. He brought you here and he will take us back home.'

'The army have gone back to Jerusalem. They're going to destroy it. How can you say we're ever going back?' Hananiah was close to tears.

'How could I know what Nebuchadrezzar dreamt? How are we still alive? There's a bigger plan, Hananiah. You can't give up.' Hananiah avoided looking at Daniel. 'You're one of my closest friends. You've been there with me as long as I can remember and when I'm in the palace, with a lot of people who resent me being there, it helps me to know that you're here, making these decisions, guiding the people. I'm so thankful that the province is being overseen by three of my friends. I know, whatever Nebuchadrezzar does next, that Babylon is in good hands. We'll help each other.' He nudged Hananiah. 'You're not alone.'

'Thanks. Have you seen the statue?'

'Yes.'

'The plinth alone is enormous. I heard that the wooden frame is complete and they're just adding the gold now. It won't be long.'

'Does it look like him?'

'You know how talented his craftsmen are! It looks exactly like him.'

Daniel shook his head. 'He's entirely missed the point.'

'The dream?'

'He's concentrating on the part he wanted to hear – the bit that focused on his own superiority – and totally ignored the rest. It's as if I never said it.'

'But I heard he prostrated himself on the ground in front of you. It must have affected him deeply to have…'

'That's the problem. In front of me. And he's heaped all these treasures on me as a reward – I just brought the message. I want him to see Yahweh.'

'Then we have to keep on. We can't give up now.'

Daniel smiled.

'Nebuchadrezzar's sending me to Carchemish to examine the astrologers and conjurers and other "wise" men there. Look after him for me until I get back.'

Chapter Twenty-four

Jerusalem

The soldiers hauled Zedekiah to his feet. His stomach turned. Dread flooded his mind so that he lost control of himself and his legs gave way beneath him. A sharp slap burned his cheek. He braced himself. He knew he was about to experience pain beyond anything he'd ever felt before. His pallid skin reflected his fear. It would soon be over. He consoled himself that it wouldn't last long.

He waited, expecting the prick of metal against his throat. It never came. Instead, he watched the knife point nearing his eye. His vision blurred as pressure built up next to the bridge of his nose. The knife slid into the corner of his eye and his head erupted with searing pain. He lost all sense of himself. Heat like a furnace burned in his eye socket. Then an agonising sensation as the metal blade slowly slid behind his eyeball, scooped it out from behind and scraped away the nerves. Zedekiah felt sticky, warm blood coursing over his cheek and down his neck before he collapsed.

They revived him. Nebuchadrezzar wasn't going to let him escape the torment so easily. They doused his head with water and slapped his face until he regained consciousness, his vision swimming and blurred and dark. Then they began again. His senses cut in and out. He saw the edge of the knife. Then darkness. Felt the pressure all over again. The burning. This time it consumed his skull. He felt as though his own flesh was on fire inside his skin. He heard a snap as his remaining eyeball was gouged from its socket. He tore at his ears, scratching and scraping to rid himself of the sound that repeated over and over in his mind. As they scraped the socket clean, nerves triggered pain throughout his body. He was being destroyed.

'Kill me!' He whispered. 'I want to die.'

Nebuchadrezzar's men did not kill Zedekiah. They bound his eyes to stem the flow of blood and left him, curled up on his side in a pool of his own urine, to experience every moment of the agony. They watched him rock himself, shivering in the endless darkness. He was reliving the last thing would ever see – the gruesome murder of his sons – and they let him.

Zedekiah's ankles were bruised. The bronze pushed down on the tops of his feet and his legs had no strength left. His toes were bruised and swollen and his feet lacerated from fumbling his way across the rocky ground. He'd lost count of how many times he'd fallen. He stopped. Exhausted breaths sputtered past his dry lips.

'I need to rest,' he said, his throat dry and his voice emerging as a rasp. 'Can I sit?'

In response, he heard the clattering of bronze links and felt his spine jar as his arms were forced forward by the shackles on his wrists. He doubled over, stumbled. His feet performed a series of tiny, faltering steps, shuffling along the uneven surface beneath him, unable to stride, struggling to keep up, to keep himself upright. He threw out his arms to balance, but they met jolting resistance. His wrists bashed against the shackles; the chain prevented them moving beyond his torso. He tilted, teetered, fell again. His forehead smashed and scraped along the stony ground, stinging and biting, tearing chunks from his flesh until they stopped dragging and jeered at his attempts to get up. He couldn't tell which way up was. He had nothing to hold to steady himself, nothing to pull on. He clutched at the air. He fell to his knees over and over again, his balance confused by the blinding pain. Their hollow laughs echoed around his head and his broken heart, and he was consumed with his own personal darkness. His senses were fighting to compensate for his lack of sight, but he was not used to relying on them and their messages seemed crude and unreliable. They came too late and all at once and he couldn't interpret the warnings until it was too late. The world was bewildering to him now. His breaths were short and shallow; his head swayed constantly in confusion and fear. The sickening pressure in his skull was compounded by every thought he tried to think. His entire body ached with emptiness, loss, loneliness and hatred. And the bandage round his face was tight, heavy with thick, congealed blood that stuck to his skin and tugged and tore at it with every movement. Zedekiah was alone. Everything was black.

A crackling sound confused Zedekiah. He wondered if it was coming from somewhere inside himself. Perhaps it was the inside of his body crumbling like weathered stone, decaying like a dry dead leaf. Perhaps it was his heart. The crackling grew louder. Faster, fiercer. Zedekiah was hit by a wave of heat.

'What is it?' he called in confusion, not sure who he was directing the question at, or even if there was anyone there to hear it. 'Are you going to burn me now?'

The laughing spiraled inside his head again, swirling, dizzying, nauseating. Was this what insanity felt like?

'We're not going to burn you.' The voice was scornful. 'It's Jerusalem.'

'No!'

'I wish you could see it,' the voice continued mocking. 'It's quite beautiful in flames. The glow is slowly consuming it. There's a bluish haze over the whole horizon. Can you see colours now, in your mind?'

'Stop!'

'The palace is almost nothing. The Temple, houses...'

'The Temple?'

'Yes. Your pathetic little temple will soon be a pile of charred rubble, but don't worry, we've taken everything out first.'

'Taken everything...' Something was wrong about that statement. Zedekiah couldn't focus. Couldn't think.

'We'll melt it down in Babylon. It'd be a shame to waste the bronze.'

'Take me away. Throw me into the flames. I don't want to be here. I...'

'We'll go soon. There's only one more thing. The whole of Babylon's army has been slashing the base of your wall with axes for this – you should feel privileged to have attracted such attention from Nebuchadrezzar. Or perhaps you were hoping to avoid his notice? No matter. It'll soon be over.'

Anger burned inside with all the heat of the flames that consumed his city. He longed to see the face of his tormentor. To scorn him with the hatred in his eyes. But he couldn't. He'd never express himself that way again.

The ground shook beneath his feet and a deafening rumble resounded through his body. Zedekiah panicked. He was being swallowed up. Consumed. The earth was closing in over him.

'And the walls come tumbling down!' And then that laugh again. The hollow, haunting laugh.

Chapter Twenty-five

Babylon

Nebuchadrezzar took his hands away from Amytis' eyes. He rested them on her shoulders and whispered in her ear.

'It's for you.'

Amytis looked at the new structure in front of her. Layer upon layer of greenery rose before her, high into the air; leaves spreading, stretching, trailing and dangling. They caught the light in intriguing and enticing ways. The whole thing was alive with possibility and promise. It softened the burnt brick structure that supported it and though it was not quite the same – it didn't have that rugged quality – it reminded her a little of the mountains of her Media.

She held Nebuchadrezzar's hand and stroked the back of it with her thumb. She led him towards the tower and he followed, enjoying seeing her so happy. She climbed the steps to the first level and wove her way through the arches to explore the plants. Amytis approached each in turn. She took time, looking closely, reaching out to touch the leaves and learn the textures, stroking them gently. She spoke the names of those she recognised, and marvelled at those she didn't, greeting them like new friends. She was enthralled. The trees were planted thickly together, exactly as if they had grown there by nature and not design. She breathed in deeply, inhaling the sweet scent of the leaves, and looked up. She wanted to see sunlight glinting through the branches – a cherished memory – and was not disappointed. Tears welled up in her eyes. Her gift was beautiful.

Amytis continued exploring and appreciating every twist and turn, until she reached the top level of the gardens. This was as high as the city walls. She looked down through the gathering dusk at the boats on the Euphrates, and out across the city.

'Nebuchadrezzar?'

'I'm here.'

'The garden is beautiful. It's exactly what's been missing.'

'You like it?'

'More than all the gold and lapis lazuli in Babylon.' She rested her head on his chest. 'It's perfect. Thank you.'

Nebuchadrezzar and Amytis sat in the garden together and watched the sun setting behind the city wall. Amytis had always believed that Nebuchadrezzar had only married her to consolidate the alliance between Media and Babylon, that it was a diplomatic move. She'd never believed he cared about her. Sitting beside him tonight, she was unable to think those things any more. This gesture was not about his dominion. For once, it had nothing to do with the kingdom. Nebuchadrezzar had commissioned this for her. He had listened to her heart and responded. Just for her. Amytis leaned her head on his shoulder and cried.

Chapter Twenty-six

Babylonian plains

The plains of Dura were crowded. Most of the population of Babylon and the surrounding villages had gathered there at Nebuchadrezzar's command. Looming over the crowd and imposing its indomitable presence on them, tall, proud and dazzling, was a golden image of the king. Even the plinth it stood on dwarfed the citizens. And from its feet above their heads, it stretched endlessly upwards to its head in the clouds. It towered high. The entire statue was covered in a thick layer of gold, so that it appeared solid and glittered brightly in the sunlight. This statement was not about Babylon, but about its king. Etemenanki stretched into the heavens, Amytis' gardens were a botanical treasure trove, the walls a defensive triumph and the processional way stunningly beautiful because of its attention to detail. Groundbreaking construction techniques had been employed throughout Babylon to defend it against the power of the Euphrates, to support and water the gardens, to build a gateway to the gods. Nebuchadrezzar was more proud of his endeavours in building the city than in any of his conquests in battle. He loved his city. Lived for it. But this image surpassed all the other triumphs. The statue of Nebuchadrezzar was the most lavish, resplendent and vain addition to Babylon so far. The statement proclaimed, 'I am Nebuchadrezzar; the greatest ruler of the greatest civilisation on earth. None will ever surpass me.'

There was a hushed reverence as people craned their necks to view the face of their king, to consider its likeness. They shielded their eyes from the glare with cupped hands or by squinting. The craftsmanship left them flabbergasted. They were awe-struck. Speechless.

When Nebuchadrezzar ordered the crowd to bow down in front of the statue to worship it, compliance was automatic. Most didn't question his authority even for a moment, or consider his request strange. Most depended on him and had been driven to greater collective achievement under his guidance and leadership. Why wouldn't they thank him? Why wouldn't they make a display of their servitude to this great man of wisdom and power? They fell to their knees and buried their faces on the ground. A sea of bodies fanned out from the foot of the statue and spread out across the plain, like ripples in water. Nebuchadrezzar watched with deep satisfaction. He surveyed the scene, scanning from one far edge of the populace to the other.

And then he stopped. The feelings of pride, happiness and self-importance that bordered on narcissism were obliterated in an instant. Rage flooded his head and swamped his chest. He was a thunderbolt – focused, angry, devastating – and ready to strike. Three figures stood within the crowd. Their conspicuous stances – glaringly contrary to the king's command – betrayed the rebellious nature of their hearts. These were dangerous men. And their insult was devastating in its intensity – because these were not just ordinary men. Nebuchadrezzar recognised them immediately. He had recently promoted them. Hot, angry blood pumped fast through Nebuchadrezzar, fuelling his fury. Their behaviour was nothing short of mutinous. He had nurtured them, taught them, given them influence. Even their names were gifts to them, high honours from his palace. And they were choosing to use all that privilege to publicly defy him. He seethed with indignation. These men represented the administration of Babylon – represented him.

Shadrach, Meshach and Abednego would suffer the consequences of their arrogance. They'd betrayed him before the entire kingdom. Now the entire kingdom would see the example he'd make of them.

Chapter Twenty-seven

Babylon

An enormous yawning archway led into the kiln. Day after day it swallowed clay bricks in their thousands, blasted them with extreme heat, and spat them out again, forever changed by the experience. They emerged newly impervious to the creeping damp of the city and shining with a glaze that would retain its lustre for all time. This was the process that made Babylon the enduring symbol of greatness it was.

Daniel hurried along the street, drawn by the commotion. He'd returned from his duties in Carchemish to find the palace empty and much of the city abandoned. His mind raced. Something was happening. Something significant enough to attract a huge audience. It could have been a celebration, but he didn't think so. The atmosphere felt claustrophobic. Ominous. He pushed through the rows of people, crammed together and clamouring, and his stomach knotted. His heart thumped. Daniel knew that something was very wrong. This scene disturbed him. He held his breath and shoved harder, desperate to penetrate the frenetic rows of bystanders, driven by the desire to find out what insanity the king was implementing now. He couldn't think – his consciousness was flooded with a sense of foreboding – so he forced through.

Daniel's stomach plummeted. He stood immobile at the front of the pulsing crowd, held back by the line of soldiers, as though a living creature had just expunged him from its belly. His chest heaved. Emotions flooded over him, mingled and confused, and paralysed him. His friends – Mishael, Hananiah and Azariah – were bound with thick cords that he knew must be biting into their skin and burning their flesh. They were tied around their wrists and ankles, unable to move, each propped upright by two enormous soldiers. Daniel couldn't get past the guard; he couldn't make his words heard above the jeering of the angry crowd that pressed in behind him. They didn't see him. But he saw the flicker of consuming fear in Hananiah's eyes. He knew that Azariah was steeling himself for the agony and understood the smouldering doubt behind Mishael's defiant tirade of sparks. He knew these men. They'd been his friends in Jerusalem. They'd been through everything together. Until now. He didn't understand. A rip tore through his centre. He looked at the gaping mouth where tiles were usually loaded into the kiln. He saw the flames through the window higher up where fuel was added – today it blazed like the eye of a demon. At the top, where the funnel usually emitted harmless plumes of smoke, dangerous flames leapt high into the air, raging. Daniel experienced a torturous range of emotion – guilt that it wasn't him, confusion, anger. But he couldn't do anything. He wasn't going in. His friends were.

'Is it true?' Nebuchadrezzar had bellowed. His face contorted with the violence of his feeling. 'Shadrach?' Hananiah hung his head. 'Abednego?' Azariah's chin quivered. 'Mishael?'

'We didn't bow.' Mishael confirmed what the king already knew.

Nebuchadrezzar's voice resounded louder with each word. 'I have appointed music on the most lavish scale, to the most beautiful standard ever heard – horns, flutes, the lyre, trigon, psaltery and bagpipe – for this purpose; that when you hear it, you will fall on your face and worship the image that I've made.' He got to his feet and moved closer to the men, making them uncomfortable. His barely audible whisper was unambiguous. 'If you are ready to do so, very well.' Then his face changed and he bellowed, making Hananiah's hands fly to his ears. 'But if you do not, you will be cast into the midst of a furnace of blazing fire. What god can save you from my hands after that?'

Mishael straightened his back, refusing to be intimidated by the king's steady gaze. 'We don't need to answer that. Our God is able to deliver us from your furnace. He will deliver us out of your hand, O King.'

'Even if he doesn't,' Hananiah said, joining the debate, surprising himself with his fresh confidence and lifting his head, 'you should know that we are not going to serve your gods or worship the golden image that you have set up.'

Nebuchadrezzar turned to one of his servants. 'Tell the commander of my army to choose his most valiant men. I need them. Also, send instructions for the kiln to be prepared.'

'Shall I have them remove the bricks?' The servant asked.

'Yes... No! Use the glazing kiln. It's hotter. And have them stoke the flames. I want them to burn seven times hotter than usual.'

Daniel could feel the wall of heat from where he stood. In the air around the kiln, the city's buildings appeared strange and distorted. He was nauseous. Rippling waves extended outward from the kiln's walls and the ground around it reflected light like the surface of the river. Daniel was light-headed. His vision faded in and out.

Tall stacks of tiles lined up outside the kiln. They must have stopped production for this. Nebuchadrezzar never stopped production. This was serious. Daniel's insides ached.

The noise swelled in the darkness. Daniel forced his eyes open. They were moving, shoving his friends down the slope towards the hungry mouth. Where was Nebuchadrezzar? Daniel swept round. Everything was blurring.

They were halfway there. Daniel howled. The sound welled up from the pit of his stomach and his lungs propelled it out of his open mouth. Agony. Nobody heard. It was swallowed by the noise of the crowd.

Pulsing. Throbbing. Daniel's head was going to explode with the pressure. He was so hot. Feverish.

Light shone through his eyelids. Swimming colours of orange, yellow and white. He made himself open them. One of the soldiers responsible for feeding the kiln was wrapped in flame. Daniel saw him and nothing else, as if dreaming. The slivers of light leapt and danced on him in front of the crowd, silencing them. All sound had abated. Babylon held its breath. In the hushed street, where even the Euphrates had faded to a respectful background whisper and the birds had fled, the soldier's screams were harrowing.

Adrenaline kept Daniel alert now. He was repulsed, but felt compelled to watch. The flames fed on the soldier's fat, wicking it through his clothes, steadily consuming him. The acrid smell of burning hair wafted through the street in bursts. The soldier plunged to the floor, writhing and screaming. He gasped. The crowd gasped. With a final shudder, the struggling stopped. His limbs splayed limply on the ground. Empty eyes stared out from his contorted face while his flesh continued to nourish the flames. Daniel forced his eyes away. He couldn't see his friends. He felt sick. They were hidden from view by the sheer mass of the other soldiers. Cramps wrenched his stomach. The other soldiers struggled. Sweat evaporated as fast as it reached their skin, rising in a steamy mist around them. Every step took enormous effort. Another hit the ground with an audible thud. He clutched his chest, choking, wheezing, gasping. Slowly suffocating.

It happened quickly after that. A chaotic chain of carnage and combustion. One by one the soldiers fell to the ground, unable to withstand the immense heat, suffocated by fumes and then ignited – human fuel for Nebuchadrezzar's insatiable inferno. Heaps of burning flesh lay strewn along the ramp. The smell was nauseating. Horrified, the crowd stood transfixed. Daniel strained to see beyond the billowing smoke and flames.

Hananiah, Azariah and Mishael were at the bottom of the slope, near the arch of the kiln. Too close to it. Daniel's mouth hung open. They were alive, but still bound. Unable to escape. Swaying. Tottering.

He watched in horror, witnessing every moment in vivid detail as Hananiah fell, taking the others down with him, and they rolled into the gaping jaws of the kiln.

Chapter Twenty-eight

Babylon

Nebuchadrezzar watched the roaring flames for a few moments longer. He rotated his shoulders a couple of times, then dropped them back down with finality. His job was done. He turned away from the kiln and was surprised to see a lone figure at the front of the crowd, sitting on a limestone slab in the middle of the street, facing the kiln entrance.

He was even more surprised to realise it was his servant, Belteshazzar. *What was he doing?* Nebuchadrezzar looked at Belteshazzar, who looked back at him. Then it dawned on him. Belteshazzar had asked him to promote these three, hadn't he? He'd known them. Now he thought about it, he knew that they'd studied together. They'd arrived together from Jerusalem. So it was understandable that he'd be mourning them. Nebuchadrezzar nodded. He felt a little sorry for Belteshazzar. He was a good man. But as he watched, another thought occurred to him and his expression hardened.

'Belteshazzar,' he said and watched Daniel hurry to his feet. 'What is the situation in Carchemish?' The guard moved aside to let Nebuchadrezzar through.

'O King, I...' he faltered. 'I... I'm sorry. I'm distracted today.'

'These were your friends.' His voice was softer than usual. Daniel nodded. 'Do you know how they brought this end on themselves?'

'King Nebuchadrezzar...'

'When your friends refused to follow my instructions they mentioned their God. Were they talking about the same God who told you my dream?'

'Yes.' Nebuchadrezzar inhaled, considering this.

'Belteshazzar, if you had not been in Carchemish, you would have bowed before my statue, wouldn't you? It was you who inspired it...'

Realisation permeated Daniel's features, but his eyes remained sorrowful. 'No, King Nebuchadrezzar. I would not have bowed.'

Nebuchadrezzar's mind reeled. He was confused. His mind dictated that he should push Belteshazzar through the mouth of the kiln immediately to join his friends. The traitor stood before the king of Babylon, admitting the same heart of treason Nebuchadrezzar had just publicly condemned. But he hesitated. There was something about Belteshazzar that Nebuchadrezzar couldn't identify. It intrigued him. There had been no hint of rebellion in his statement. It was factual. Nothing more. Nebuchadrezzar looked beyond Daniel. Most of the crowd were dispersing, returning home to relive the execution with vivid retellings, but a few near the front lingered, keen to see how this new conflict would develop. *What's wrong with me? Just get on with the job.* But Nebuchadrezzar liked Belteshazzar. He was exceptionally talented, a wise and faultless servant. *I'm being too soft.* His God had done what no other could. The same god that...

'They told me their God – your God – could save them from the flames.'

A smile spread across Daniel's face. 'Yes. He could.'

'But he hasn't, has he? Your God is not real.' Nebuchadrezzar turned away. He needed to think. He stormed back past the guards, towards the kiln and stared into the flames. He shouted to the guards.

'How many men were thrown into the furnace?'

'Three,' one replied.

'Look at this! Come and tell me what you see.'

The guard hurried to join the king and peered down into the flames which, though quieter than before, still raged within the kiln. He looked at Nebuchadrezzar.

'Well?'

'O King, forgive me. My eyes trick me. I know that there were three men and that by now all that is left is a heap of their bones, but I see four men. I see them walking around inside the flame. Forgive me.' He hung his head.

'Then I am not losing my mind.' Nebuchadrezzar leant forward and shouted down. 'Come out!'

Chapter Twenty-nine

Babylon

'I don't understand,' said Amytis. 'One minute everyone is bowing down in front of a giant golden statue of you, at your insistence, because they feared for their lives if they didn't...' She slumped back against the cool tiled wall. '... And the next, you're making a total fool of yourself in front of all your officials – governors of Babylon, magistrates, administrators – blessing their God, the one that caused them to refuse you in the first place!'

'Yes, Amytis. That's exactly what happened.'

'But what must they think of you now? You're swaying this way and that like a reed in the breeze. They expect you to be strong and upright like the statue. Unbending. They must think you're losing your mind.'

'And for the most part, I am—'

'Losing your mind?'

'—strong and upright. But... Amytis, my officials were there. They know I didn't just imagine this. They saw that the bodies were intact, the clothes were not even singed...'

'Really?' She leaned forward.

Nebuchadrezzar stopped pacing and looked at her. 'Yes. That was what was so amazing. My soldiers died in the heat – it just devoured them – before they even got close to the kiln opening, but these men fell all the way in and were entirely unharmed.'

Amytis let herself slide down the wall until she sat on the ground. She folded her arms around her knees and tipped her head back to rest on the tiles.

'Only their God could have done that. They didn't even smell of smoke.' Nebuchadrezzar crouched down. His tone became conspiratorial. 'Amytis, I think it was him in the flames with them. Or an angel. I saw four figures moving in there and the extra one wasn't human.'

'You're going mad. Did the heat affect you? Have you had enough to drink today?' She reached out to feel his forehead. He let her.

'It was like a son of the gods. It was there, speaking with them, protecting them. And when they came out, they were unbound. So, either the cord burned, without leaving a single mark on their skin, or someone unbound them.' His eyebrows were raised, inviting Amytis' opinion.

'I don't know what to think. What does it all mean?'

'It means, Amytis, that I have made a new decree. I understand it all now. This God has given me power and wealth and sent me incontrovertible signs. He made me influential because he... needs me. It all makes sense. In the dream Belteshazzar interpreted there was an everlasting kingdom – their God's kingdom will be the everlasting one! So, I have made a decree. I, Nebuchadrezzar, king of Babylon, have a responsibility to defend this God before the people.'

'Any people, nation or tongue that speaks anything offensive against the God of Shadrach, Meshach and Abednego shall be torn limb from limb and their houses reduced to a rubbish heap. There is no other god that is able to deliver in this way.'

Nebuchadrezzar had addressed the crowd directly. His scribes had been present to ensure that the decree was recorded and distributed accurately throughout the kingdom. Nobody in Mesopotamia would miss this communication.

'Nebuchadrezzar the king to all the peoples, nations and men of every language that live in all the earth: May your peace abound! It has seemed good to me to declare the signs and wonders which the Most High God has done for me.

How great are his signs
And how mighty are his wonders!
His kingdom is an everlasting kingdom
And his dominion is from generation to generation.'

'You should rest,' Amytis said. 'It's been an emotional day.'

Nebuchadrezzar nodded. He made himself comfortable in a chair and rested his head on his hand. He was asleep before Amytis had brought a sheet to cover him. But his sleep was fitful again, and he slumped lower in his chair with every anxious turn. Amytis sat by him and listened to his troubled muttering.

Chapter Thirty

Babylon

'O King, live forever. I only wish this dream referred to somebody else. If only I could tell you it was meant for your enemies.'

Daniel walked with Nebuchadrezzar in the palace courtyard. He had been called in when none of the other wise men of Babylon had been able to supply the meaning of Nebuchadrezzar's latest troubling dream. He looked at Nebuchadrezzar, who remained quiet. Daniel knew that the king trusted him. He wouldn't be here if he didn't. But he didn't like what he knew and he knew that Nebuchadrezzar wouldn't either.

'I call you Belteshazzar, according to the name of my god, but,' he hesitated, 'I know that a spirit of the holy gods is in you, Daniel.' Daniel looked up, surprised to hear his Judean name used after so long.

'No mystery baffles you. Please tell me how to understand this dream. It scared me and I'm still afraid when I remember it.' Daniel turned his head away. He closed his eyes. A hand rested on his shoulder and the king spoke again. 'Don't be troubled by the dream – it's not meant for you. I know your God is sending me another message. You're not responsible for what's in it and I don't blame you. I just need your help.'

Daniel bit his lip, looking at Nebuchadrezzar. He nodded. 'The tree – growing larger and stronger, with branches stretching to the sky, beautiful leaves and abundant fruit – is you. The tree is visible to all the earth because you are known everywhere. Animals live under the tree's shelter and birds nest in its branches and all of them are fed with the fruit it supplies.'

Nebuchadrezzar stopped walking. He watched Daniel, and listened intently.

'You are the tree. You have grown strong and powerful. Your dominion reaches to the ends of the earth and your Babylon provides everything the people could possibly want.'

Nebuchadrezzar stood on the roof of his palace and looked out over his city. He inhaled and stretched his arms high. When he lowered them his chin was high, his shoulders back and his chest proud. He was satisfied with what he'd achieved here. More than that, he was feeling smug about it all. The restoration of Etemenanki was almost complete. Its walls had been strengthened and lavishly decorated with low relief depictions of the gods and the staircase was fully repaired. All that remained was for an additional tier to be added to its height – it would surpass all expectations of what was possible in engineering – and for Marduk's temple to be installed at the new summit in the clouds. Amytis' gardens had thrived in their home. The plants had established themselves as a significant feature of Babylon's landscape. Amytis had been right that the city had needed a touch of the natural world to soften its dramatic outline, but Nebuchadrezzar took all the credit for integrating the foliage so well with the solid baked brick structure and implementing the whole concept on such an unrivalled, majestic scale. Nebuchadrezzar watched his industrious citizens going about their business. He saw the smoke from the furnace, the boats travelling in and out of the market dock and the horse-drawn chariots speeding around the city wall. He looked at the beautiful adornment along the processional way – the ultimate showcase of skilled craftsmanship. He saw the sun glinting from the blue glaze that proliferated in the design of his most important buildings. His fond gaze lingered on the golden statue beyond the city wall. Nebuchadrezzar smiled at the harmony of it all. He couldn't think of anything more perfect than Babylon. His Babylon.

He laughed aloud, sipping wine from a goblet, and, driven by ecstasy, shouted from the rooftop, 'Is this not Babylon the great, which I myself have built as a royal residence by the might of my power and for the glory of my majesty?' He lifted the goblet above his head.

Nebuchadrezzar's stomach knotted. He clutched himself as he folded in the middle. The goblet clattered on the floor, spilling the wine which ran in rivulets across the roof terrace. His pain was severe. He screwed up his face. Anxiety and fear consumed his mind and body, causing every part of him to become taut and edgy. A voice – otherworldly and disturbing – spoke directly to him. He knew nobody else could hear it. He knew he had lost control.

'King Nebuchadrezzar, to you it is declared: sovereignty has been removed from you, and you will be driven away from mankind…' He knew the power of this voice had overwhelmed him. He couldn't fight it. Nebuchadrezzar's body was out of his control.

Chapter Thirty-one

Babylon

Amytis screamed. The shrill note splintered the peace in every chamber of the palace. She stumbled backwards, staring at her husband. She didn't know him. He was scaring her.

'Nebuchadrezzar, stop! Please stop.' Her face was wet with the tears that fell from her eyes. She couldn't see clearly. 'Stand up.'

Amytis clutched her hands together in front of her body to control her shaking. She tried to focus her thoughts, decide what to do. She wanted this to end. She wanted Nebuchadrezzar to comfort her. But not while he behaved like this.

The king snarled. His upper lip curled up at one side. Inside, his teeth were clamped together. Saliva pooled in front of them and dripped from his mouth in a long glutinous string. Amytis shuffled further back. She kept her wide, confused eyes on him, terrified. Her husband was transformed. Nebuchadrezzar was on his hands and knees. Angular knuckles bent his fingers into claws and his nails tapped and scratched at the tiled floor. His back arced upward from his solid shoulders. His legs stretched to push his body forward. He was more animal than human. But the most dramatic change was to Nebuchadrezzar's eyes. They were narrow, focused and empty of understanding. They had lost all their humanity. Nebuchadrezzar leaned to his right and tilted his head. He clawed at the air with his left hand and growled. The low, guttural voice hit Amytis in her stomach and made her nauseous. She shrieked back at him.

'Stop it. Get up. You're scaring—'

Nebuchadrezzar bounded forward with bestial strength. His muscular legs propelled him through the air and he landed at Amytis' feet, crouched low, snarling, ready to pounce. Amytis kicked him and spun away. She ran across the room and clutched the back of the chair, shielding herself from her husband. Her eyes were wide and her heart racing. What had he become? Nebuchadrezzar turned, a creature scorned, and leapt toward her again. He tore through the room, knocking furniture and treasured figures to the ground around him. Amytis' ears were filled with clattering and smashing, but the terror of his growl persisted. A table fell, ensnaring the beast. It howled.

There was a moment of quiet while the creature licked its wounds, distracted. Absorbed momentarily in its own pain. Amytis sidled out from behind the chair and crept toward the door. Survival was instinctive. She ignored the pain in her heart, brushed aside her aching concern for her husband and tiptoed away, tears streaming down her cheeks. The only thing that mattered was to get out of the room alive. Hardly able to see the floor through her tears, Amytis stepped on a small statue of Ishtar, goddess of love, and felt the crack. She froze. The creature cocked its head. It had heard too. Amytis fled. She ran toward the door as fast as she could. It wasn't far. But the creature vaulted onto her shoulders. His knees slammed into her back and she fell, face first onto the limestone. She felt her forehead crack against it. The room blurred and swam. The colour faded. Nebuchadrezzar had her pinned to the ground, his full weight pressing through her torso, pressing her stomach into the ground. She stretched out an arm an attempted to drag herself along, but she couldn't lift herself. The beast clawed at her hair, her neck jolted back and felt like it would snap. Her skin was taut and strained. Her throat tight. It yanked hair from her burning scalp in clumps and her head flopped forward again. Her forehead hit the stone again. Her head throbbed. As the claws came at the side of her face, tearing strips from her skin, Amytis screamed again, longer and louder in her desperation than ever before. She felt the blood, warm on her face. She tried to breathe, but her lungs were being squeezed and each shallow breath hurt her chest. With one final effort, she pushed against the weight, determined to throw it off, but she succeeded only in lifting the beast slightly, unsettling it and provoking more growling and scratching.

As the room faded into darkness, Amytis heard distant footsteps. They were rushing. She hoped they were coming. She hoped the pain would end. She closed her eyes.

The guards thundered through the doorway. They stopped inside the door, arrested by the strange sight, confused by the scene, uncertain what to do. Their presence disturbed the beast and it fled, parting them like wind through the fields. Safe from Nebuchadrezzar's wrath, one crouched to lift Amytis. Another found a chair in the debris and righted it. They placed her there. They looked uncertainly at one another. This situation was out of their usual experience.

'Find Belteshazzar. He'll know what to do.'

Chapter Thirty-two

Wilderness

Nebuchadrezzar emerged from the crevice in the rock. A shadow fell across his face. He moved along, careful to remain under its cover. It was dawn and the sun was surfacing at the horizon, but he preferred to stay close to the outcrop. He didn't belong out there in the light. He didn't belong anywhere.

Nebuchadrezzar clawed at a stone in the dust, scraping his long yellow nails across the scratchy surface. They were thick and crusted and curled over his fingertips in sinister arcs. He flexed his fingers, lifting his nails from the surface before dragging them over it again and again and again. The sound grated in his ears, but he couldn't stop. His body had made him a passive observer. He was constantly subjected to the pain of his own actions but he'd long ago given up any attempt to control his bestial body; it simply wouldn't respond. Nebuchadrezzar longed for the return of that glorious ability – to connect his mind and body again – something he'd taken for granted for so many years. Until it had been snatched from him in that single moment on the roof.

His mind drifted from that memory to Amytis and, lifting his face to the sky, tears welling in the corners of his eyes, he howled. The note was haunting. It hung around him. He hated it. In the distance a donkey brayed, warning him. *Stop*, he willed himself. *Be quiet.* It was futile. He felt his chest expand as he inhaled and his jaw pushed itself forward to shape the sound. A second howling note, longer and louder, forced its way out from within him, ringing out across the plain. Nebuchadrezzar's heart was beating against his ribs. Sweat beaded on his forehead. He was aware of what he'd done to his wife, and he grieved her pain every day. The braying came again. He ached inside, desperate to hear that she was unharmed, that she understood, forgave him, missed him... He heard the hooves. He felt panic. Couldn't contain the energy. His hind legs propelled him forward across the dust. It was sticky with dew and stuck to his hands and knees as they pounded the ground. They were close. He circled the rock, panting and drooling. Then he flicked his head in the other direction and bounded in a smaller circle as if chasing his own tail. He caught a glimpse of a wild donkey blurring past. It was too close. He had to get away. Run! He commanded his legs. Run! But his legs weren't obeying him. Nebuchadrezzar's matted, dangling hair entangled itself around his limbs, his chest jolted against the snag, and his face collided with the ground. He closed his eyes as he felt his arm yanking, forcing itself free, tugging at the thick rope of hair which tore at his scalp. He focused, willing his arm to stop. Longing for the self-destruction to end. That's when he felt the punch in his ribs that took his breath away and saw through his wavering vision the hind legs of the wild ass preparing for its next kick. Even the wild donkeys of the Mesopotamian plains had not accepted him, base as he was. They were solitary creatures and defended themselves well. He was entirely alone and all his growling and snarling did not fool them. He was man. A man deranged, but still a man.

Nebuchadrezzar didn't know how long it was since he'd fled Babylon, though he had memories of it. His skin was bronzed and tough as leather, his eyes bloodshot. His whole body responded like an animal. The torture came from his mind, which seemed – to him at least; he had nobody else to ask – lucid and coherent, and yet was so utterly ineffectual. Nebuchadrezzar had only the monotonous routine of his day, dictated by animal instinct and uncontrollable urges. He had one now. Despite all the pain of his injury, his limbs carried him out onto the plain in search of good grazing. Nebuchadrezzar shuddered. A storm rumbled in the distance.

Chapter Thirty-three

Babylon

Amytis stared out of the window. Babylon seemed empty without Nebuchadrezzar. It was still the same place. The impressive structures remained as daily reminders of his achievements. The council of prominent nobility ensured the smooth running of the city. Trade relationships had been maintained, agriculture was monitored so that everybody throughout the kingdom continued to eat well, festivals were held according to their proper schedule and rituals observed. But for Amytis, Babylon had lost its heart. The great king above all other kings had brought life to this city. He'd instigated new research and cultivated new thinking. He'd kept the landscape evolving and changing with his building programmes. He'd created an excitement, shared by everyone who lived within these walls, at being part of this glorious culture. Amytis ground her teeth together. This stagnant version of Babylon felt more like a monument to her husband than a thriving centre of culture. Policy concentrated on maintenance now rather than development. Even the army had switched their default mode of operation to defence. But Nebuchadrezzar wasn't dead. She narrowed her eyes, detesting every citizen who had let themselves forget. It was so easy for them. Unresolved anger still ate away at Amytis. She had tried to distract herself with various tasks, occupying her mind with gardening or art or literature – she'd even had the officials teach her how to fish – but nothing brought her joy. Nothing brought her the closeness to Nebuchadrezzar she longed for. Everything was meaningless now.

Amytis still had so many questions about what had happened to Nebuchadrezzar. She tortured herself every day, replaying what she knew, hoping for new revelation.

'Amytis?' Daniel crouched in front of her, holding her hand. She saw him there, but couldn't focus. Her vision faded in and out. She knew that she had gashes on her face and that a physician had cleaned them. The preparation had stung her and she'd screamed and fought. She knew that guards had lifted her into this chair and before that something abominable had happened to her. Every time she closed her eyes she saw a terrible beast, vile and depraved, and she shook uncontrollably. The beast had her husband's face. Where was he? Why wasn't he here?

'Nebuchadrezzar!' she shouted. She forced her eyes open and cast around. She only saw Belteshazzar. 'Nebuchadrezzar!'

'Amytis.' She was shaking. 'Amytis, look at me.'

'Where's my husband?' She ripped her hand from Daniel's.

'Amytis, Nebuchadrezzar is unwell.' She inhaled sharply. She must go to him. Amytis pushed herself up, but her legs were weak. She was dizzy. She collapsed back into the chair and breathed. She considered the Judean her husband had promoted – he'd trusted, relied on and, she suspected, liked this man more than anyone. She knew this was rare. Most people were afraid of her husband and gave him only what he wanted. This man was different. He'd always said what he believed the king needed to hear, without a thought for his own life, wealth or reputation, and Nebuchadrezzar had respected his honesty and integrity. He'd often mentioned these unique qualities to Amytis. He'd been grateful for them. She trusted Belteshazzar to tell her the truth now too. She burned to know what was happening, but she felt sick. The image of the beast flashed into her mind again. What was that grotesque vision? Why did she keep seeing it? Her eyes begged Belteshazzar for an explanation.

'He knew this would happen.'

'But…' she was confused. Nebuchadrezzar hadn't said anything to…

'There was a dream. I interpreted it for him.'

Amytis nodded. She was listening.

'In his dream, he was a great tree, but a holy one came down from heaven and shouted, "Chop down the tree and cut off its branches, strip off its foliage and scatter its fruit."' Daniel swallowed. 'He said the animals would flee from under its shelter and the birds would fly out from its branches. Your husband would be drenched with dew and… and eat grass like an animal.' Amytis gasped. She shook her head, holding back hot tears. Daniel spoke gently. 'The holy one said, "Let his mind be changed from that of a man and let a beast's mind be given to him." Amytis, I'm sorry.'

'Why didn't he tell me before…?'

'I don't know.'

'Why didn't I know?'

Amytis hid her face in her hands and sobbed.

She turned away from the window, tired of the depressing scene, and wiped the tears from her face with the back of her hand. She sniffed. She stretched her arms high into the air, willing herself to feel enthusiastic about the day. To feel anything. The numbness was killing her.

Amytis saw something move on the periphery of her vision – a flicker of changing light as if a shadow had passed across the room. Her chest tightened. She forced herself to breathe. Something was in the room with her. She felt it there. An image of the beast appeared in her mind, memories of that violation, the shattering of her trust... It was happening again. Slowly, she turned toward the door. She breathed deliberately and forced her eyes to remain open. When her shoulders and feet had turned to face the threat, she brought her head into line with them. She was trying to act more bravely than she felt. She told herself she'd fight if she had to, but inside she was preparing to run. At first she didn't see anything. She'd been foolish. She was imagining things.

But it came. Out from the shadows beyond the door, the bulk loomed larger, shifting silently, until it entirely blocked the light. Amytis froze.

Chapter Thirty-four

Babylon

The beast was back. It was worse than Amytis had remembered. Her frame shook. She didn't move from the spot. She didn't scream. Fear held her prisoner, paralysed with perturbation. A strain of music repeated over and over in her head, sweet, innocent, completely incongruous. It didn't help. Her palms were sweaty, her senses were alert and each breath caught in her throat. She was scared.

The beast had thick, tangled locks of hair protruding from its face and head. They were matted together in heavy strands that hung over its shoulders, down its body, to its middle and then thinned and frayed in straggling, wiry strings. Glimpses of its hide showed through; rough, dark and mottled with discolouration. Sharp talons splayed across the floor from its feet and hung ominously from its hands. Were they hands? The beast stood on its hind legs, human in its stance, but in every other way animal, fierce, wild, primal. Amytis could taste the foul odour and swallowed hard, trying to dislodge it. She gagged and bent forwards. She didn't vomit. Forcing her eyes back to the beast, Amytis righted herself. She stepped backwards, creating space between them, concentrating on a plan. She didn't expect her thoughts to be interrupted. And the voice was not what she expected to hear. She'd expected growling, snarling, ferocious, frightening noises. But not words. Not that voice. Soft and gentle and understanding.

'Look at me, Amytis.'

'Get out! Get away from me.'

'Please look.'

She looked. Her husband's voice had unnerved her. She hadn't heard it for… but it couldn't be real. She was delusional. The beast was unsettling her mind and she was imagining things. She looked at its form. Utterly inhuman in every aspect of its posture, bent and muscular in all the wrong places, animal-like even in this standing position. But as she squinted and looked harder she wondered. Could it be human? Beneath the dirt and the accumulated toughness and neglect, was there a human who'd lost sight of his own nature, who'd forgotten how to stand tall and proud? She looked at the bloodshot eyes and her body jolted with recognition. Behind the bloodied whites was an expression she knew well.

'Amytis.' The beast stepped into the room. It took small steps, attempting to make itself submissive and unthreatening. 'The most high is ruler over the realm of mankind. He bestows it on whom he wishes. No one can ward off his hand. I know this. He has done this to me because of my pride and...'

Amytis shook. She wept. Nebuchadrezzar moved towards her. She knew it was him. The words he spoke were unfamiliar and sounded wrong on his lips, but his voice was unmistakable. Her heart longed to run to him and be comforted, but she couldn't bring herself to get close to this monstrosity. She despised it. Hated everything it represented. Amytis let out a cry of lament and hurried past him, out of the room.

Chapter Thirty-five

I remember Nebuchadrezzar as human. No different from anyone else. He was king of Babylon, with a kingdom that spanned all Mesopotamia, and was burdened with the pressure of his position; he made decisions with epic consequences, was brutal in battle and ruthless in trade; he left a legacy that will last for generations. But first he was a man. Nebuchadrezzar had the same flaws and weaknesses as the rest of us. He had questions that went unanswered, haunting fears and doubts, insecurities. Yahweh used him anyway. He chose Nebuchadrezzar to deal with the arrogance of the Judeans and destroy the desecrated Jerusalem. He spoke to him about the future. Yahweh took the king of Babylon on a journey from disbelief to complete dependence, dealing along the way with his self-importance and inability to understand. It cost him his dignity, but he emerged from the experience saying, 'I, Nebuchadrezzar, praise, exalt and honour the king of heaven, for all his works are true and his ways just, and he is able to humble those who walk in pride.'

Nebuchadrezzar began as my captor and master but became my friend. I was pleased to serve Nebuchadrezzar, and grateful that Yahweh gave me that opportunity. I was older, and had learned from my experiences too. Faith for the little things affected the culture of Babylon much more than I'd believed possible. Yahweh had protected me. He'd protected my friends. We'd sought the welfare and prosperity of Babylon, and Yahweh allowed us to prosper with it. I was excited for the future. I still had many years to live here. Babylon would remain my home a while longer; I had built my house and planted my garden. Now was the time to cultivate it.

Part 3

Belshazzar's Babylon

'A lion has gone up from his thicket,
And a destroyer of nations has set out;
He has gone out from his place
To make your land a waste.
Your cities will be ruins
Without inhabitant.'

Chapter Thirty-six

The years after Nebuchadrezzar's death were unsettled ones for Babylon and I found myself praying continually as I completed my work in the palace. Nebuchadrezzar's son, Amel-Marduk, took the throne. As a king, Amel-Marduk had strong convictions and followed them, but he didn't nurture diplomacy like his father had and so he lost the support of his citizens. Nebuchadrezzar had found the perfect balance between maintaining the admiration and respect of his people and instilling an edge of fear, but Amel-Marduk failed to appreciate the benefits of this. He neglected to be generous. Against my advice, he also began reforming his father's policies while the citizens were still grieving their former king. Amel-Marduk believed Jehoiachin's 37-year imprisonment had been unjust and released him in a deeply unpopular move. Jehoiachin was given one of the highest positions in Babylon and regularly dined with the king. I saw the people turn their backs. It was not long afterwards that his own brother-in-law, Neriglissar, orchestrated Amel-Marduk's brutal murder. Nebuchadrezzar's son had survived only two years and Neriglissar ruled for only four. When his son, Labashi-Marduk succeeded his father, he was still a young boy and, despite my nurturing, proved utterly incapable of ruling the vast and complex kingdom of Babylon. Nine months after he took the throne, another conspiracy culminated in a second murder and shook Babylon's confidence again. The security and strength that Nebuchadrezzar had built into the fabric of the city, which kept harmony among the multitude of citizens in the vast area they occupied, was being steadily undermined from within.

Nebuchadrezzar's lineage, both by blood and by marriage, had now been exhausted. No suitable heir to the throne remained. This was a critical time for Babylon and I prayed daily for Yahweh's protection. Eventually the people settled on Nabonidus. He wasn't Chaldean, so his selection heralded a new era for Babylon.

The city held its breath in anticipation of great things.

Chapter Thirty-seven

Babylon

Nabonidus was still talking, no doubt explaining important details, but his son, Belshazzar, wasn't listening anymore. He'd heard everything he needed to know. He tried to look solemn and nod in the right places, but inside he was bubbling with excitement. He was elated. He battled to contain the grin that was desperate to burst out and begin the party.

'Belshazzar?' He snapped his eyes back to his father's face.

'Yes?'

'You have been listening, haven't you? You seem distracted.'

'I apologise, Father. I admit my mind was diverted… reflecting on the weight of new responsibility I'll have to bear.'

His father smiled. Belshazzar thought he saw a touch of relief on his features. Good. That's exactly what he'd hoped to achieve.

'You'll rise to the task admirably. I know you will. I've not yet left and you're already preparing yourself for the pressure of the position.'

'Father, who will advise me in your absence?' Belshazzar suppressed a smirk.

'My counsel will remain in Babylon. And you may send a messenger as often as you require to Taima.'

'Will you be away for long?'

'It is hard to say. I plan to establish a significant trade centre and ensure the routes remain uninterrupted into the kingdom. It may take some time. I certainly don't intend to return until after the spring festival next year.'

Belshazzar forced a straight face. 'Then there will be no festival. It can't happen without you here.'

'I know. The people will have to do without it. I have more important matters to deal with. I don't understand why Sin has been neglected here. I'm going to rectify that, but Marduk is really not that important to me. '

'He's everything to the Babylonians, Father.'

'Then I'm proud to call myself Assyrian.' Belshazzar saw Nabonidus cast a sideways glance at the guards. They were professional enough not to respond, but Belshazzar suspected it had irked them. He'd have to get them on his side. But now, he'd put a few finishing touches on his stellar performance.

'Father, you'll be gone so long? I…'

'I believe I can trust you to take care of the concerns I have outlined. You have proved to me that you're ready.'

'I'm pleased you think so. I'll do my best to live up to your expectations. I intend to make you proud of me.'

Nabonidus chuckled. 'I already am, Belshazzar. Just remember that you are not alone in this task. Seek advice constantly. The counsel here have been advising for years – think how well they served Nebuchadrezzar. They know what they're talking about and you will do well if you heed their advice, just as I do. Listen to them, particularly with regard to the security of the kingdom. There are nations who think us weak since Nebuchadrezzar's death, and are looking to take advantage of that.'

'I'll do that.' As Nabonidus strolled past him, Belshazzar rolled his eyes.

Nabonidus clapped Belshazzar on the back and swept out of the throne room. Belshazzar waited until he had left and then sprung high into the air. He landed, and spun around with arms stretched wide and a grin on his face. He laughed.

'Crown Prince, forgive me, I...' began one of the guards.

'Quiet!' Belshazzar barked. 'I won't be disturbed now. I'm celebrating my impending freedom.' The thought of it made him laugh again. He was alive with energy.

He liked the sound of his new title: Belshazzar, crown prince of Babylon...

... and co-regent.

Chapter Thirty-eight

Babylon

The chariot careered along the processional way, swaying dangerously to one side and then the other. The horses neighed in fear, echoing the screams of the people as they dived out of Belshazzar's way. He howled with laughter.

'Faster!' he demanded. 'Faster!'

Belshazzar embraced the rush of cool air across his face. A thrill of fear travelled through his body as the chariot tilted to one side, tipping him off balance and prompting gasps of horror from those nearby, before righting itself again. That momentary doubt he felt for his safety made him feel alive!

Belshazzar swigged from the flask of wine he clutched in his right hand.

'Stop!'

The horses' hooves skidded along the limestone tiles as the driver tugged abruptly on the reins. The chariot, driven by its forward momentum, only came to a standstill when it collided with their back legs, causing them to rear up in pain. Belshazzar laughed again.

'Take me to the river.'

The driver did his best to calm the animals while suppressing his own stress. Today's escapade meant that another four of his horses would be too spooked to work again. If the prince continued undermining the horses' training at this rate, the army would soon have to reduce the number of their teams. He seethed. It was senseless cruelty and waste. Sensing Belshazzar's impatience, he hauled himself back onto the front of the chariot and took up the reins. Belshazzar clapped him on the back so hard that he almost fell from his position. Wine splattered over his tunic.

'The river!'

The driver clenched his teeth.

'I have a family!' the nobleman protested. 'You can't do this!'

Belshazzar smiled. 'But you see, I've already decided. It's only fitting for the equal ruler of a city like Babylon to have multiple residences. From this one by the river, I will be well positioned to oversee the trade that occurs here.'

'With due respect,' he muttered something under his breath, 'it is customary for new residences to be constructed for the purpose.'

'Would you have me waste this nation's time and resources?'

'No, of course...'

'I'm sending my men this evening. You will have the house and gardens vacated by then or they'll forget to be polite.'

The man stared vacantly for a moment. Belshazzar watched the realisation dawning on him. 'Where will we go?'

'You'll find a little mud-brick dwelling, sufficient for your needs. If not, you could try constructing something yourselves. You can hardly need more than one room.'

Belshazzar looked beyond the man to the vast baked-brick residence. It was beautifully maintained and elaborately decorated and the garden stretched right down to the Euphrates. He was satisfied. This was the perfect place for tonight's celebration. His father had written from Harran to say that he was detained restoring the temple there to Sin and would not progress to Taima until he'd overseen its completion. He hadn't even asked about the situation in Babylon. Belshazzar was free to continue doing his own thing. He just had time to acquire a few outlying estates for his own personal provision before this evening.

Chapter Thirty-nine

Babylon

Mishael sat in his official room in the temple complex, poring over the figures. The situation was bad. He'd sent word to Nabonidus months ago about the state of the treasury, but the accounts kept arriving and the amounts involved were growing. He pressed his forehead with the heel of his hand. The thought of having to raise taxes any further perturbed him. Babylon was already furious about the king's lack of accountability for his extensive restoration works. Resentment at his absence from the capital was widespread and their inability to confront him irked many prominent businessmen in the city. And then there was the scandal of his son's blatant abuse of power and squandering of every resource he could lay his hands on. Mishael sighed. He was uncertain how to proceed with this. He needed Daniel's advice.

Hananiah closed the door. He had heard enough. He got up from his chair and stretched his arms wide to try to return some feeling to his weary body. He paced. He was frustrated with this constant feeling of helplessness. He'd never felt so unable to make a difference to the people's lives as he had since Nabonidus had taken the throne. Since then, his day consisted of hearing complaint after complaint and issuing apology after apology for having his hands tied. In every aspect of society he was unable to change matters for the better. His heart grew steadily heavier and his mind was tired. He was little more than a receptacle for the outpourings of Babylonian discontent. Just this morning he'd heard at least four separate stories of how Nabonidus' heavy-handed reforms had negatively affected industry and craftsmen in Babylon. The people felt neglected. They felt Nabonidus' heart lay elsewhere. Hananiah suspected they were right. He gathered up his records and set out to find Daniel. He'd have some sage advice. And if nothing else, seeing him would make Hananiah feel better.

Azariah completed his inspection of the vaults. He couldn't understand what was happening. In the past week, supplies had diminished by more than twice their usual level. This rate of consumption was unsustainable. Despite every mechanism he'd put in place to protect against famine, Babylon was still edging dangerously towards it. Azariah had carefully regulated the rationing of provisions. He'd briefed everyone who worked for him about the situation, but they were tight-lipped under questioning. He knew it was Belshazzar and his interminable entertaining, but it would help if his team weren't being bribed to help him get away with it. The crown prince was single-handedly jeopardising the health of the nation. To make matters worse, fewer and fewer ships were arriving at the market. This was harder to explain, but Azariah suspected the new camel caravans at Harran had something to do with it. Nabonidus was redirecting the best of the resources, paying only lip-service to the capital. And with this downturn in prosperity, Azariah was noticing an increasing neglect of public areas and residential streets. People were losing the incentive to care. In the past rising levels of rubbish in the streets were always dealt with, covered over with fresh clay and allowed to set in the heat. Now, the mounting debris of daily life was simply abandoned. It was filthy and, Azariah was certain, contributing to the rise in illness in the city. This situation was getting out of hand. Azariah needed to take it to a higher authority. One who would listen. Daniel.

'I've spoken with Belshazzar more than once. He refuses to listen.'

'Daniel, if anyone can make him see what he's doing, you can,' said Azariah. 'You always know what to say.'

'The crown prince doesn't want to take advice from anyone. Least of all me.'

'Why?' asked Mishael, his brow was furrowed.

'He knows I'm from Jerusalem. He gloats about it.'

'But Babylon destroyed Assyria too.'

'I know,' said Daniel. 'Belshazzar does too.'

The four looked at each other. Their youthful skin had gained the roughness of time and lines had developed on their maturing faces. They saw less of one another with all the responsibilities of their positions and the particular pressure of these days, but the bond between them was still easy. They all understood the silence that fell between them now. They waited for Daniel.

'Belshazzar knows his father's policies are unpopular. With Nabonidus' long absence, he could easily have seized the throne, but it has eluded him. Belshazzar has some skill and experience with military strategy but beyond that...' Daniel trailed off. Mishael nodded. They understood.

'He would rather indulge in the luxury of his position than learn the skills of a great leader but I think he despises himself for it. He aspires to be a great king. He just can't change his habits. And by now, he'd also have to work hard to change public perception of himself. Insulting me is a good outlet for his frustration. I'm an easy target. But my job is to serve him. So that's what I'll continue to do.'

'And you'll bring our concerns before him? Azariah asked.

'Continually.' Daniel gave his friends his word.

Chapter Forty

Persia

Cyrus granted the emissary an audience. He was intrigued. What could Nabonidus have to say to him? He ordered food and drink for his unexpected visitor and invited him to sit.

'Greetings from Nabonidus, King of Babylon.'

Cyrus nodded.

'Nabonidus has heard of your triumph in battle over the Medes in their capital. He is aware that you have risen to power in Persia.'

'These things are true.'

'King Nabonidus respects you greatly and wishes me to make known to you the extent of his great power.'

'I am already aware of your king.'

The emissary hesitated. Cyrus thought he looked uncertain. That was fine. Cyrus didn't want to give anything away until he understood the purpose of this visit. He waited for his guest to compose himself.

'You are aware of the extent of the Babylonian kingdom?'

'Indeed.'

'King Nabonidus would like to propose an alliance. He feels that the combined forces of Babylon and Persia would be unrivalled in influence. He believes such a relationship would be advantageous to both parties.'

'Where is Nabonidus now?'

'In Harran.'

'In Harran?'

'Yes.'

'According to reports from my army, there is a Median presence in Harran.'

'That is correct.'

'And the Babylonian army has not suppressed it?'

The emissary cleared his throat and glanced down. 'No...'

'That is interesting. It has been most enlightening to meet you. Please, stay a few days as my guest. I will ensure you are well provided for while I consider my response.'

The emissary scrambled to his feet and bowed. Cyrus left, his mind racing through the new information he had gleaned from that poor, naive messenger. He was certain that Nabonidus had not meant for such a revealing picture of his weaknesses to be painted. Still, there was no use feeling sorry for the man. Nabonidus would deal with him on his return. Cyrus knew that his job was to analyse the information he'd received, however unintentionally it was given, and act in his own best interests.

He summoned the commander of his army, a former governor of Assyria who had defected to join him. He was now one of his most loyal and trusted friends.

'Gubaru, we have interesting news.'

'I'm ready to do whatever you require, Cyrus.'

'Excellent. First, King Nabonidus appears to have abandoned his capital city. I will need you to find out who he has left in command and ascertain the temperature of the city.'

'Certainly. My men will be dispatched before the end of the day.'

'Only a few. We must remain inconspicuous.' Gubaru nodded. 'And secondly, Nabonidus himself seems to be having trouble with a small band of Medes in Harran. This leads me to suspect he is not in full control of the enormous military resources at his disposal. I don't think he knows what he's doing.'

'Are you sure? The Babylonians have long been a force to avoid upsetting. Their dominion is unrivalled.'

'Yes, but I have the distinct impression that his own interests are not military. He sent an emissary to propose an alliance, but offered no indication of what he would lend our cause. I think he's asking for help in this field.'

'Do you wish me to dispatch a portion to assist him?'

Cyrus shook his head. 'With respect, an alliance with Babylon could be immensely profitable. Their trade relationships are the most lucrative in the region. They also attract tributes from far and wide. I've heard boasts of their riches. We could request a high price for your military expertise.'

'Or we could acquire it all.' Cyrus had a faraway look.

Gubaru's eyes widened as he realised what he'd just been asked to do.

Chapter Forty-one

Babylon

Belshazzar staggered down the narrow steps to the vault. He shuddered. It was cold and dark and the walls seemed to be leaning in towards him. He blinked several times, trying to get his vision back in its proper perspective, but in vain. His was dizzy and slightly nauseous. Why were these steps so narrow? Belshazzar pressed his hand along the brick wall to support himself. The cold shocked his clammy palm. He shivered. The vault keeper had gone ahead with the flaming torch and Belshazzar was in near darkness. He thought about calling out but decided against it. He hated to appear weak and needy. He hated the secret fears that haunted him; darkness, enclosed spaces, unnatural heights, water, failure. The list was long and shameful, but Belshazzar had never admitted them and he wasn't going to now. He had his way of coping. His fingers tightened around the flask as he thought about it, reassuring himself it was there if he needed it. He looked down. Everything beyond the next two steps was shrouded in shadow. He slid his foot forward, searching for the edge of the step by the feel of it. He knew he couldn't rely on his eyes. Not when the walls were moving – his head didn't believe it, but the illusion was frightening – and when wine was pumping round his body, Belshazzar's heart was gripped by terror again. His foot slipped off the edge and his body jolted downwards. His heart was in his mouth. So was a large amount of regurgitated wine. It burned his tongue. He leaned over and expunged it from his lips, wiped his chin with the back of his hand and swallowed the foul tasting residue. He washed it down with a long swig from his flask. He breathed in and out, then took a second swig.

A halo of light emerged at the bottom of the stairs, growing steadily brighter as the vault keeper returned. Belshazzar strolled down the steps with a casual nod and took control.

'Where have you been storing the gods?'

'If you'll come this way, I'll be glad to show you.' Belshazzar stayed close this time. The floor was uneven and beyond the reach of the flickering flame of the torch as the keeper forged further and further forward. Shadows loomed large and shrank away, throwing distorted images around in the semi-darkness, playing tricks on Belshazzar's already straining eyes. He had no concept of how large this vault was. It seemed to extend eternally in every direction. Each step forward revealed new images; statues and vases and bowls. Strange curves and eerie eyes drifted in and out of view. Belshazzar was relieved when the keeper spoke again. 'Here.' He spun to the left, throwing a shaft of light along a row of statues laid out on the ground. They looked like dead bodies, Belshazzar thought. He stared at them, squinting, seeing rotting flesh and exposed bones where none existed. His imagination was vivid and he could smell the stench of decaying matter. He swallowed down another mouthful. 'These are the ones that arrived in the last week.'

Belshazzar nodded. 'I anticipate there'll be plenty more. My father wishes to protect them all. He takes this duty seriously.'

'Forgive me, is there a threat?'

'King Nabonidus believes so.'

'But I have heard of no military intervention being prepared in Babylon. My son is a soldier. He hasn't mentioned...'

'There is none. I have not instigated defensive measures because I don't believe they are necessary. Babylon's refusal to accept Sin as the rightful superior to Marduk has affected my father deeply. He is devoted to the moon god. I humour him with regard to this, but no force can threaten us. Who is there able to challenge Babylon?'

'With respect, we should deal with every threat, no matter how small. Never underestimate anyone. That's what Nebuchadrezzar...'

'Don't speak that name!'

'I…'

'You tell me my job and then insult me with such a comparison! I am ten times the ruler he was.'

'My apologies,' muttered the keeper, who looked sideways at Belshazzar. 'It won't happen again.'

'It is likely that he will continue to send gods from the temples wherever he travels, for their "protection". Have you space to accommodate them in an orderly manner? My father insists on order.'

'I have. I intend to move this collection…' He turned to face the other direction. A shaft of light travelled through the blackness at speed, upsetting Belshazzar's balance. '… To a separate chamber, to create space to keep the gods in one place, in the sequence in which they arrive. That will make it easier to restore them to their homes when the *alleged* threat has passed.'

Belshazzar narrowed his eyes. He suspected the keeper was questioning his judgement on the matter. But he would let it go. The threat was alleged. He'd hardly needed to interrupt his renowned partying to consider the matter. There was nothing more to it than the wild imagination of an old fool. Something else had his attention though. This strange little collection of articles now thrown into light by the torch ignited his interest. He couldn't think what it was about them, but they held his gaze. Excitement welled up in his chest.

'What is this collection?'

'It's the spoils from the Temple in Jerusalem. Articles from their temple. Sacred artefacts. Whatever they used in their rituals, I suppose. No gods though. I've always thought that was odd.'

'Before you rehouse this, bring it all out. I need an exact inventory of what's there. And then I want it cleaned up...'

'Certainly.' The keeper sounded uncertain.

'... and weighed.'

Chapter Forty-two

Sippar

Cyrus stood on Babylonian soil. He stretched and smiled as he looked across the plains. A caravan of camels formed a silhouetted line in the pale early light on the horizon. Trade had flourished here for years because the routes were safeguarded by the all-pervading security of the kingdom. As long as Babylonian cities controlled the land across which they travelled, bandits could not get close enough to steal the precious resources. They would continue flowing in to the capital. Cyrus was a long way from Babylon itself, but this was the first step in unsettling the system – and its effects would be felt. That emissary from Nabonidus had truly been a gift. The Medes had been an easy target and Cyrus now had the added benefit of the combined forces of the Persian and Median armies at his command. He gave his commander the signal.

Gubaru and his men approached the small city of Sippar. He sent a few ahead, unarmed and bearing a tribute to Nabonidus, who had arrived here in his quest to protect every sacred image in Babylonia. Since he'd already recruited the Medes and massacred the inhabitants of Opis, Gubaru wasn't at all convinced his tactic would yield success, but the gates opened, and the rest of his men charged in.

Gubaru had charged into the fray. He'd drawn his dagger from its sheath while running and slashed the air at his left and right. He was an intimidating figure. The war cry rose from deep in his chest and received an immediate echo from the rest of Cyrus' men: the immortals. They were here to make their presence known in Babylonia. Opis on the river Tigris was just the beginning. But what a beginning! Gubaru found himself face to face with a Babylonian soldier. He didn't hesitate. He plunged his dagger deep into the soldier's throat and kicked his legs out from under him. As he cast around, assessing his next move, Gubaru gave the dagger a flick, sending globules of brilliant red blood raining down on the writhing body of the soldier. With his left hand, Gubaru brought his spear to a horizontal position, fending off swords with clamourous clashing. He was alive with the thrill of battle. Sweating, gulping air into his lungs, and fighting to the beat of his heart. He jabbed his spear hard into the stomach of the next soldier, flinging him backwards to the ground. Babylon retaliated by slashing at the end of his spear until the tip had been sheared off. Gubaru spun the spear in a dizzying arc, until the back end had replaced the tip. The golden lizard sticker glinted in the bright light of the day.

It denoted his rank, but had a more practical purpose. He plunged it deep into the gut of the next man to draw near. The battle didn't last long. The Babylonian faction at Opis was small and ill-prepared. The advantage of surprise was on Cyrus' side. Gubaru's skill at leading his men on the battlefield was matched by Cyrus' excellence in planning and strategy. They were an unstoppable team. Gubaru dealt the final blow himself. He had felt a strike to the small of his back. Someone had broken through, behind him, and his men had failed to intercept. Gubaru spun around, grateful for the little scales of bronze that layered the leather coat he wore. He knocked the sword from the lone hand with the first blow. Looking into the eyes of the Babylonian, he grabbed his bow from his shoulder, drew an arrow and placed the tip on the soldier's forehead. Then he took ten paces backwards. The man didn't move. He was surrounded by Persians and Medes. He had nowhere to go. The arrow hurtled through the air and pierced a perfect hole in his head. He fell slowly to the dust, blood spurting, groaning and gurgling. The voice of Babylon was silenced and a cheer went up from Gubaru's immortals. Their number was intact.

And then, the inhabitants revolted. They came at the immortals with anything they could find. Gubaru had no choice but to order a massacre. He stood back and watched, shaking his head at the folly. It was a waste.

But they'd forced his hand. Gubaru led his men away from Opis and the scene of devastation and death. The city ran with blood. Ribbons of red rippled in the Tigris. The dead littered the streets like the rubbish they'd deposited beneath the clay. Gubaru's heart was heavy. That had not been part of the plan.

But the massacre lent the immortals sway at Sippar. Their legend had travelled on the wind and arrived before them. No one put up any resistance. The city was seized without a battle. Nabonidus fled.

Chapter Forty-three

Babylon

Raucous laughter filled the air in the palace courtyard. Belshazzar had exhausted the potential of his countless new estates. He had partied hard and enjoyed the company of the pre-eminent members of Babylonian society, but he felt his influence waning. People were tiring of the monotony. It seemed that even ultimate luxury to the point of decadence became tiresome over time. Belshazzar's notoriety was fading, slipping through his grasp, and he was becoming desperate. He had to make this evening different. It had to be unforgettable. The palace was the only appropriate venue for something on this scale and Belshazzar was about to cause a scandal. He'd always loved a touch of drama – it was just what was needed now. But Belshazzar hadn't bargained for the dramatic turn of events this evening would provide.

Babylon's best musicians played lively tunes. The pace and dynamic was increasing as the evening wore on. Noblemen and officials danced and swaggered, putting aside all their usual decorum, and bellowed to air inane thoughts over the hubbub. The space was crammed with bodies. There were more in attendance than at any previous event Belshazzar had hosted. A thousand nobles were present. A thousand would witness Belshazzar's premeditated spectacle. He was back at the top and loving every moment. He tipped his cup to his mouth and poured the wine in, allowing it to spill out of the sides of the cup and dribble down his chin. He wove his way through the crowd, smiling and laughing jovially, receiving the admiration of the nobles for the success of the entertainment, monitoring the mood. As Belshazzar watched inhibitions drop, lewdness spread like an infection and all pretence of civilisation and politeness fade away, he could hardly contain his excitement. Belshazzar was deliberately biding his time.

This was it, Belshazzar thought. The time was perfect. The sun was low in the sky, the crowd were at the peak of their wine-induced euphoria, and he couldn't wait another moment. He leapt onto the platform at one end of the courtyard. The musicians broke off abruptly in the middle of an energetic melody, causing temporary confusion in the crowd. Belshazzar waited. Eyes turned to him; chatter turned to hushed whispering and faded until all that remained was the occasional drunken giggle.

'Let's feast!' Belshazzar signalled for his guests to make their way to the interior of the palace where tables had been prepared. Torches burned brightly in stands around the perimeter and lavish arrangements decked the walls. When everyone was seated, Belshazzar stood at the head of the foremost table and raised his glass.

'The vessels from which you will be drinking tonight have been liberated. They have spent too long in dark and dingy storage and have not been put to proper use.' A cheer erupted, echoing from the walls. When the rowdy applause had died down, Belshazzar continued in a stage whisper. 'In confidence, these vessels are best suited for this purpose – the drinking of wine – but that was not their original one.' He paused, allowing the question to form in the minds of his guests, building the suspense and loving the attention. He leant forward. 'To me a sacred vessel – one that might be used in a temple – should be more... In Babylon, our gods receive infinitely better. Our craftsmen spare no detail, our treasury denies no price for the service of our gods.' Nods of agreement and national pride greeted the crown prince in response to his words. 'Hold your vessel in you hand. Look at it, closely. Is this sufficient? Is this the best?' He paused again as many followed his instructions.

'In Jerusalem, the answer was apparently "yes"!' A hush descended in the room. Every eye was fixed on Belshazzar and there was a discernible collective intake of breath. 'In Babylon, they will hold the wine and satisfy the appetite of mortals. So drink!' Belshazzar sat.

There was a nervous pause as his words sank in and the nobility pondered whether this was some kind of trap. Did Belshazzar really expect them to do this? And then somebody laughed and broke the tension and suddenly the golden chalices from the Temple in Jerusalem were being raised and clinked and used as if it were perfectly normal practice.

'To Marduk, supreme ruler of the gods!'

Another voice echoed, 'And to Ishtar, may she grant us love and fertility.' A chorus of agreement erupted.

'May Baal cause the sun to rise in the morning, when our feasting is over.'

'And we praise Shulpae for the feast!'

The shouts were coming faster and louder.

'Ninatta, bring us more music.'

The noblemen were working their way through the gods of Babylon, who stood on ceremony around the room. They'd begun with those fashioned from gold, adorning the front wall, the focal point, but they were moving down through those made of silver, bronze and iron. Even the simplest, made from wood or stone, were not overlooked. No god was excluded for fear of incurring their wrath and spoiling the party. The toasting had become a game, and laughter accompanied every new suggestion.

'To Siduri, we thank you for this excellent wine.'

Belshazzar's feast was under way. He smiled.

As the co-regent ate the food that had been offered to the gods in Babylon's temples – the finest and best the earth could produce and a privilege enjoyed only by royalty – the atmosphere changed. Belshazzar stopped chewing. The room was quiet. Unnaturally quiet. He looked up from his plate. His guests had stopped eating. They were staring. What was wrong? His plan had gone so well. But now they looked worried. Fearful. His pulse quickened. He turned to see what held their attention. Belshazzar swallowed. He doubled over. He was choking. The meat he'd forgotten to chew was lodged in his throat. He could feel it there, like a huge boulder in the tiniest stream. He coughed. He couldn't breathe. His eyes were wide and his face was pale. He coughed again. He felt a hand clap hard between his shoulder blades. Once. Twice. It was still there. And a third time. The meat leapt into the back of his mouth and Belshazzar expunged it onto the floor. He gasped for breath. His throat felt odd – as if the lump were still there – but he could breathe again. He uncurled from the waist, raised his head and looked again. It was still there. He hadn't imagined it. In front of the plaster wall of the palace, looming large, strangely disembodied, transparent and yet unmistakably clear, alive but otherworldly, hovered the back of a hand. Everyone could see it. The hand was perfectly formed. Belshazzar glanced at the back of his own and then back again. The texture of its skin was real, lined and creased and darkened by the sun. He stared. Swallowed. Felt himself sweating. Its veins protruded as its fingers moved, curving round as if to hold something. What did this mean? What was it doing? Belshazzar stepped back and collided with the table. Golden chalices tipped and spilled their contents. Wine ran to the floor in streams. He clutched the edge of the table for support. He was shaking now. The hand moved up the wall. The suspense was agonising. Uncertainty consumed Belshazzar and he felt exposed. The hand continued moving. It drifted over the surface in smooth lines like the hand of a craftsman. It left its mark. Strange letters were appearing. Belshazzar had seen something like them before – another language – but…

'Is it the hand of Nabu? Is it a message from the gods?' The voice shook, afraid of the words it spoke. Belshazzar felt his knees give way and braced his arms harder against the table to support his weight. Beads of sweat gathered on his face. He shook.

The message was complete. Four words were written on the wall, in large, perfectly formed lettering. The torches burning in the stands beneath it illuminated the words for all to see. But Belshazzar was perplexed. He could not read the words. And nobody was forthcoming to help him. He looked foolish. Anger rose up within Belshazzar; his forehead burned with the passion of his feeling. His event had been interrupted, undermined and taken over. He'd been publicly wronged. He propelled himself to his feet and spun around to face the cowering guests.

'Any man who can read this inscription and explain its interpretation to me shall be clothed with purple and have a necklace of gold around his neck, and have authority as third ruler in the kingdom.'

His offer was generous, but his voice betrayed his threat. Belshazzar's face glowered with barely concealed rage.

Chapter Forty-four

Euphrates

Cyrus plunged his shovel into the ground again. He leant on it with all his weight and dug. This was back-breaking work, but he was not above getting his hands dirty. Time was not on his side. Cyrus had a large team of Persian and Median soldiers with him north of Babylon, beyond the sight of the city's sentinels, and the immortal thousand under Gubaru's capable command were depending on them.

Cyrus looked up. A wide straight channel was emerging. They had begun in a tiny stream and dug in a line towards the mighty Euphrates all afternoon, heaping the soil in a mound that ran along one side of their canal. Lines of 20 men, side by side, dug in layers. The first 20 removed the dry topsoil, those following behind dug a little deeper and each line behind increased the depth still further. Military order was critical if they were to succeed. The sun was now setting and the men were tiring. The channel was deep. It needed to be. Although Cyrus knew in his heart that it wasn't deep enough, he would never discourage his men. In all likelihood the water would burst the banks of the newly constructed canal and flood the land. If it didn't, it would certainly overwhelm the stream on its winding way to the Tigris. But that didn't matter. It could be repaired later, and a small repair job was vastly preferable to the cost of the years they would need to spend encamped around Babylon's impenetrable walls if he were to lay siege to the city. The food surplus there, though his sources informed him was depleted, could feed a nation for a ridiculously long time. No – this was his best option, and secretly he had high hopes for it. Cyrus had found Babylon's weak link.

'Everybody out!' Cyrus yelled. The thick wall between their canal and the course of the Euphrates was beginning to show the strain. The earth was flexing like hot metal. It could give way at any moment. His men scrambled to obey the command. Shovels lay abandoned on the damp, claggy earth. Those on the banks extended their hands, pulling and heaving their men up the steep incline, while others pushed from below. Cyrus looked on with pride. At this moment, his men were noisy and chaotic and showing signs of panic, but they were functioning as a perfect unit. No man rested until the whole group was clear of danger. Those without a specific task coaxed and encouraged and offered suggestions until the last man flopped, stomach first, onto the dust at the top of the bank and grinned. His legs still overhung the edge, but he used his arms to drag himself forwards, his body slithering in snake-like curves as a cheer went up that Cyrus suspected could be heard from Babylon, it was so loud. The men hugged and punched each other's shoulders, received hearty claps and jumped in celebration. They felt a surge of energy at the completion of a task that had consumed their efforts all day.

The ground creaked, and they scurried to the bank to watch. The entire team lined the bank, craning their necks to see. The earth groaned again under the pressure of the water. A crack appeared at the top of the bank, zigzagging rapidly down its height. The first droplet emerged. A trickle began at the top, seeping, dribbling, then pouring into the empty channel like water from a jug; a round, clear stream. It hit the bottom, generating a fine spray and an ethereal rainbow, swirled around in a growing circle, then set off on its winding course towards the stream. It had travelled only a few feet when the bank of the Euphrates gave way, exploding through the remaining earth and deluging the canal. The men jumped back to avoid the spray. They laughed and cheered. Cyrus' soldiers sprinted alongside, revelling like children in the simple joy of the moon's silver light, dancing and tripping over the undulating surface of the cascade. Before, brown earth. Now, a glorious body of water.

Chapter Forty-five

Babylon

Belshazzar's pride was shattered. The man standing before him – the only man in the whole of Babylon able to answer his challenge – was in exile from Jerusalem. The very place he'd belittled. The insult stung. It was bad enough that an old woman had been admitted to the party to make the suggestion. He'd been reduced to publicly taking advice from his mother-in-law. He wished the ground would swallow him up. His reputation – and he'd been so close to restoring it tonight – lay in tatters. And now he was metaphorically bowing to the superior wisdom of a captive. His world was upside-down and out of control. This went against every fibre of his being. He aimed for a heavy note of disdain in his voice.

'Are you that Daniel who is one of the exiles from Judah, whom my father the king brought from Judah?' Belshazzar had hoped for a laugh, but received none. The guests were distancing themselves from him.

Daniel inclined his head in affirmation.

'Now I have heard about you that a spirit of the gods is in you, and that illumination, insight and extraordinary wisdom have been found in you. Just now the wise men and the conjurers were brought in before me that they might read this inscription and make its interpretation known to me, but they could not declare the interpretation of the message.' Belshazzar admitted this through gritted teeth.

Daniel waited calmly. Belshazzar turned up his nose, pained by addressing his own words to this outsider.

'Now if you are able to read the inscription and make its interpretation known to me, you will be clothed with purple and wear a necklace of gold around your neck, and you will have authority as the third ruler in the kingdom.'

'Keep your gifts for yourself or give your rewards to someone else; however, I will read the inscription to the king and make the interpretation known to him.'

Belshazzar's eyes flew wide. He tilted his head and tightened his lips in warning. This Daniel had omitted the customary greeting – the respectful words that, although Belshazzar was not technically king, he fully deserved as co-regent and had come to expect. It had not gone unnoticed. And he had scorned the gift. *How dare he?* This man's behaviour was immoral.

'O King,' Daniel began deliberately. 'The Most High God granted sovereignty, grandeur, glory and majesty to Nebuchadrezzar your forerunner.' He emphasised the success of the former king of Babylon heavily. His disregard for Belshazzar was plain. 'Because of the grandeur which He bestowed on him, all the peoples, nations and men of every language feared and trembled before him; whomever he wished he killed and whomever he wished he spared alive; and whomever he wished he elevated and whomever he wished he humbled.' Belshazzar had asked for an interpretation and was receiving a historical tirade. He was being deliberately compared to the greatest king Babylon had ever known. This was uncalled for. It was unfair – nobody could live up to that. He riled, but he bit his tongue. He needed to know the meaning of those words. However much it hurt, he needed this man.

'But when his heart was lifted up and his spirit became so proud that he behaved arrogantly, he was deposed from his royal throne and his glory was taken away from him.' This was getting personal. Daniel had challenged Belshazzar. He was clever. Indirect, but unmistakably clear in his meaning.

'He was also driven away from mankind, and his heart was made like that of beasts, and his dwelling place was with the wild donkeys. He was given grass to eat like cattle, and his body was drenched with the dew of heaven until he recognised that the Most High God is ruler over the realm of mankind and that He sets over it whomever He wishes.'

Belshazzar stepped towards Daniel. He was overstepping himself now. Belshazzar looked around for a guard, but none came to his aid. Everyone paid rapt attention to Daniel's words as if their substance was the source of life.

'Yet you, his son, Belshazzar, have not humbled your heart, even though you knew all this,' Daniel was labouring the point now. Had Belshazzar not been humiliated enough this evening? 'But you have exalted yourself against the Lord of heaven; and they have brought the vessels of His house before you, and you and your nobles, your wives and your concubines have been drinking wine from them; and you have praised the gods of silver and gold, of bronze, iron, wood and stone, which do not see, hear or understand. But the God in whose hand are your life-breath and all your ways, you have not glorified.'

Something snapped inside Belshazzar. Suddenly, he understood. Nabu hadn't sent those words. There was a higher being involved in this. And though Daniel insulted him, he had insulted the God of Daniel infinitely more. Belshazzar slumped to the ground and trembled as he listened.

Daniel read the words effortlessly. 'MENE, MENE, TEKEL, UPHARSIN. MENE: God has numbered your kingdom and put an end to it.' Belshazzar held his breath. 'TEKEL: you have been weighed on the scales and found deficient.' He gasped and cast around. This was outrageous. 'PERES: your kingdom has been divided and given over to the Medes and Persians.'

Belshazzar hung his head. It was over. He mumbled orders and the servants clothed Daniel with purple robes and put a gold necklace over his head and Daniel was proclaimed equal third ruler in the kingdom of Babylon. What did it matter now anyway? Belshazzar's dignity had been cruelly torn away from him. He had nothing more to lose.

'Carry on!' He instructed the astonished guests. 'Eat. Drink.'

Chapter Forty-six

Babylon

Downstream, Gubaru and the immortals waited in the shadows. They could hear the revelry inside the palace, though they were separated from it by two formidably high and thick walls. Gubaru watched the water level outside Babylon slowly recede and knew that the first part of Cyrus' plan had succeeded. It was a pleasing start. But there was nothing he could do except wait. Thanks to a few strategic plants, there was a growing faction of pro-Persians within the walls. And thanks to this group, who were more than happy to assist the downfall of Nabonidus – a king who'd incorporated both tyranny and abandonment into his reign to date – and his despicable son, Gubaru had a fairly well-developed idea of what was happening in Babylon tonight. The timing couldn't be more perfect.

The water level subsided at a sedate pace. This brought the added advantage of subtlety. On a night when revelry was the primary concern inside the walls, a steady decline in the river should easily go unnoticed. Avoiding detection remained Gubaru's main concern. A sudden, dramatic change to the river would be much more noticeable and therefore a greater threat to his men. Yes, slow was preferable, but the wait was still a nervous one. It gave too much time to think about what was coming – too much time to anticipate flaws in the plan. Potential problems reared up in the minds of the waiting men. Gubaru kept a deliberate calm countenance. He examined the coil of cord at his feet. One end of it was attached to a float, which they'd placed on the surface of the river and was now sinking gradually deeper towards the river bank. When the cord had been entirely let out, Gubaru would know that water was lower than the enormous gates that secured the breach in the walls caused by the Euphrates. The Babylonians had designed the gates to extend deep into the river to prevent anybody swimming into the city beneath them. Gubaru knew this. He knew their exact dimensions. Nothing in his power was left to chance.

The first of the immortals scrambled down the soggy bank and dropped into the knee-deep water with a resounding splash. He froze. Gubaru held his breath. He signalled the men to stay still. He listened. Hoping that it had been less obvious the other side of the walls and in the towers, or that it had been masked by the noise of Belshazzar's antics, they waited to see if anyone would come to check. Until Gubaru was satisfied, nobody moved. When they did, everything happened swiftly. The first man lay on his stomach, threw his legs over the edge and eased himself backwards, supported and lowered in quietly by the one already in the water. Another two followed, then four, eight, escalating rapidly until none remained on the bank. All one thousand men stood on the bed of the mighty Euphrates. Gubaru waded through the water, feeling it flow around his calves, its warmth spreading through his body, and took his position at the front of his men. Without a word, they shifted into formation. Row after row of the immortals stood in the river, facing the gate, which towered higher from their new vantage point. They moved in harmony with the flow of the Euphrates, wading forward, feeling their footing, wading again. The Euphrates measured their pace so that the entrance resembled a royal procession. Gubaru's troops, in unknown numbers, like the waters of the river they replaced, marched at his side. Persian and Median soldiers sauntered under the proud city defences as if taking a lazy afternoon stroll rather than executing a midnight raid. The ease of the breach made a complete mockery of the massive walls. Every sword stayed in its sheath, and their shields hung superfluously at the men's sides, because the rain of arrows never came. They processed past the first wall unchecked, and then the second.

And they were in.

Gubaru was a little unsettled by the stillness of the city and the simplicity of the campaign. He had anticipated that the streets would be quiet and the security would be reduced in the light of Belshazzar's festivities, but they had met no resistance at all. *Where was the night guard? Why was nobody monitoring the river gate?* Then he saw them. A lone pair of Babylonians patrolling the street. They saw him. And his army. Inside the impressive, impenetrable walls of Babylon, having achieved the impossible. Gubaru watched realisation dawn as they took in the level of the river. They didn't signal for help. They didn't resist. Instead, the two guards nodded their acquiescence with wide eyes and sealed lips, and put down their weapons. Gubaru led his men to the steps near the market and up to the street. The Babylonians, under his instruction, directed a proportion of his men to strategic locations on the wall. Everything was easy. Key elements of the plan fell effortlessly into place.

The remaining men ran along the street from the bridge near the market, to the processional way and past Etemenanki. Their target was in front of them. One final flourish and Babylon would be in the hands of Cyrus. Gubaru ensured he had every entrance covered, and then stormed the palace. The scene that greeted him was not what he had expected. Small groups of solemn faced noblemen huddled together, muttering and shaking their heads. They looked up, surprised at Gubaru's presence and scattered. He stood in an archway and watched them swarm in disarray. They flew around the cramped space, criss-crossing this way and that, swerving to avoid one another, sidestepping, skidding, stumbling to an eventual standstill. They were trapped. The guards present drew their swords, but a lack of planning and numbers meant their attempt was short-lived.

Belshazzar sat alone at his table, a golden chalice in one hand, a silver one in the other, swigging from them alternately. A collection of empty jugs lay strewn around him. He raised a chalice to Gubaru as he approached and laughed maniacally. He rocked forward and back. Gubaru took no pleasure in plunging a sword through the pit of his wine drenched stomach and pulling it up through his chest to his chin. He performed the task unceremoniously, his expression blank and his eyes glazed. Belshazzar's entrails spilled out onto his lap. Blood and saliva dribbled from the corner of his mouth. His head flopped forward. His end was as messy as the life he'd fashioned for himself.

The nobility were released from the palace and the city continued its life uninterrupted. Belshazzar had been murdered but Babylon barely noticed.

Chapter Forty-seven

When I was a young boy in Jerusalem, there was a prophet named Jeremiah, who had brought a message from Yahweh about the 70 years the Judeans would spend in exile. I had listened with rapt attention and had never forgotten his words. Those 70 years had passed. I had served six separate rulers in that time and I now found myself adapting again to the rule of Cyrus, king of Persia and Gubaru, the governor he'd installed to supervise Babylon. Gubaru was known among the citizens as Darius – commander.

Babylonian society found itself liberated from the harsh control of Nabonidus and the citizens were freer than they'd been under any other leader. Cyrus greeted his new citizens warmly. He had an attitude of letting be, which allowed him to conquer cities throughout the region and bring them under his rule, while leaving the finer points of government well alone. Tolerance reigned. He felt no need to change the belief systems or administrative procedures that existed before his arrival. No ceremony was missed in the changeover period. This won him much popular support, and when he reinstated the festivals that had been suppressed under Nabonidus and arrested the former king on his return to Babylon, he became a hero among the people. He cemented this status by ordering the return of the gods from the

Babylonian vaults to their rightful homes in the temples of the outlying cities.

But though Jeremiah had spoken of the demise of Jerusalem at the hands of Nebuchadrezzar all those years ago, he had also predicted that he would restore the fortunes of his people and bring them back to Jerusalem to possess it again. I was not surprised when Cyrus pronounced the release of all captives. Judah was finally free of Babylonian control as I had known must soon happen. And when they left Cyrus, in his generosity, sent with them the resources they needed to rebuild the Temple in Jerusalem.

I was thrilled to see the fulfilment of this prophecy for my people but I didn't leave Babylon. It had been my home for many years and would remain so. My job was to serve Gubaru, who'd been appointed by Cyrus to lead Babylon. Yahweh had placed me at Babylon's heart for a purpose. The ruler of Babylon needed Yahweh's wisdom for this nation. It was my job to offer it.

And Cyrus and Gubaru needed prayer. Babylon had not yet seen the realisation of all Jeremiah's prophecies. But it would.

Chapter Forty-eight

Babylon

'What are we going to do?'

'We? About what?'

Two of Babylon's newly appointed commissioners huddled in a dark doorway within the palace, carrying out their whispered exchange in the shadows.

'Daniel. Gubaru chose three of us. We're supposed to be equally important.'

'We're supposed to share the responsibility.'

'Yes. But the leaders all look to him.'

'He's good at what he does. He knows what he's talking about. They respect...'

'I'm good at what I do.'

'Yes. Of course. I meant...'

'Perhaps Daniel's not as good as everyone thinks.'

'Sorry? I don't...'

'Well there must be something he isn't good at. A responsibility he neglects, or maybe he's abusing his influence for personal gain – another agenda? Something. He is human. All this generosity and humility and... What's in it for him?'

'I actually don't think there is anything. Daniel is... Daniel.'

'We'll see.'

Daniel returned to his room after a long day, listening to the concerns of Babylon's leaders, offering advice and guidance and, where necessary, gentle correction. He enjoyed his work, and was pleased that Gubaru had recognised his service to previous kings and allowed him to retain this position. He was pleased that he had the trust and confidence of the 120 leaders of Babylon and glad that his reputation among them was untarnished. He was also pleased to have two other commissioners alongside him. The accountability they afforded one another was an important safeguard in such an influential job. Consensus must be reached before change could be brought, ensuring decisions were taken in Babylon's best interests. One or two were easily corruptible; more than three could be difficult to unite to achieve any purpose, endlessly discussing and failing to decide. Gubaru understood this from his years as a military commander. He was right to have chosen this number.

Daniel knelt down at the window that faced towards Jerusalem.

'Yahweh, you are God. You keep your promises and you remember your people. Thank you for Cyrus. Thank you for bringing him to liberate your people from Babylon and returning them to their home. As they rebuild Jerusalem, help

them remember King Josiah. Let them tell their children and their grandchildren stories about their time here so that the lesson will not be forgotten. Yahweh, protect Jerusalem from corruption so that it will not turn away from you again. I can't bear the thought that these 70 years were for nothing. I long for a city built on strong and true foundations.'

Daniel continued pouring out his heart to Yahweh. He prayed, as he regularly did, for the welfare of Babylon, his influence on the culture inside the walls, and Babylon's influence in the region beyond. He prayed, like every day, for Gubaru.

'I think you were right.'

'How so?'

'Daniel. I asked everyone. I've got nothing.'

The commissioner shook his head. 'I didn't think you—'

'He annoys me.'

'He annoys you?'

'Yes.'

'Daniel isn't an arrogant man. He only likes to help. Where's the problem?'

'He's too... perfect. Doesn't it irritate you? It makes me look bad. I'm not bad. I'm not, but how can I...?'

'It's his God. He's devoted. He believes his God wants him to serve Cyrus and he does it faithfully. I think it's sweet.'

'His God.'

'Yes. His God. Yahweh.'

'That's the answer.'

'Wait. What are you…?'

Gubaru stood on the roof of the palace, looking out over the city. He liked it here. He'd been warned repeatedly of the fate of Nebuchadrezzar in this spot, but he ignored that. He came here for the quiet, the space to think and reflect away from the bustle of the palace and the long list of duties that confronted him there. Nothing grander than that. He heard footsteps behind him and turned to see Cyrus. He greeted him with a smile.

'I hear good reports on my return. You are managing my city well.'

'Thank you. I have help. My commissioners provide excellent counsel and manage the army of leaders responsible for every aspect of the city's administration, Daniel especially.'

'You distinguish one?'

'He distinguishes himself, Cyrus. I merely observe it. The man has a spirit like nothing I've ever encountered. He discerns the truth of a situation, and gets right to its essence… and he does it with the utmost respect for the dignity of the person he's addressing. I admit, I've come to rely on him rather more than the others.'

'Then he must be recognised for his outstanding contribution. Publicly.'

'Yes. You are right. Though he has no personal ambition. He isn't hungry for power.

'Which makes him even more remarkable?'

'Yes. Yes, it really does. Men like Daniel are rare.'

Cyrus and Gubaru stared into the distance, each lost momentarily in his own thoughts. Gubaru reached his decision.

'I will appoint another to fill Daniel's role as commissioner in Babylon. He is too good for the role. I will promote him above the three.'

'Promote him, but not to rule the three. From what you say of this man, we should not limit his influence to just one city. Promote Daniel over the entire kingdom.'

The two commissioners stood before Darius.

'Darius, live forever! All the commissioners of the kingdom…' He received a sideways glance from his friend and returned it with a meaningful glare. '… the prefects and the leaders, the high officials and the governors have consulted *together*,' – he emphasised this word – 'that the king should establish a statute and enforce an injunction that anyone who makes a petition to any god or man besides you, O King, for thirty days, shall be cast into the lions' den.'

Darius was distracted. He was thinking about his conversation with Cyrus and was keen to set the process in motion for Daniel's promotion. He also had a long list of tasks to get through this afternoon. The commissioner thrust a document under his nose. Darius looked up in annoyance.

'Now, O King, establish the injunction and sign the document so that it may not be changed, according to the law of the Medes and Persians, which may not be revoked.'

Darius sighed. He pressed his seal into the clay and waved them away. He was sorry that he would no longer be dealing with Daniel about matters like this. With Daniel, the experience had always been pleasant. He shook his head as he watched the two leave the room. They thought too much of themselves.

Chapter Forty-nine

Babylon

Gubaru stood at the gate, looking in. The game reserve was large, but currently housed a generous supply of lions. One looked back at him from behind its thick, healthy mane, and all Gubaru could see were its powerful jaws. He shuddered. If only he'd been a keen hunter, there wouldn't be so many. But he knew it wouldn't have made any difference to Daniel. It only took one. Gubaru's hand shook as it rested on Daniel's shoulder. His face was pale and haggard. His heart ached. What was he doing? Daniel hadn't done anything wrong. He was the most loyal man in Babylon. Gubaru blamed himself entirely for not seeing what his commissioners were plotting. He held himself personally responsible for Daniel's impending death, and he'd tried everything to prevent it once he'd realised the scheme. They'd tied him in knots. The gamekeepers rolled the enormous stone to one side and Daniel walked through.

'Your God whom you constantly serve will Himself deliver you.' Gubaru didn't know if he believed it, but he needed to say something. He had betrayed his friend and he needed to believe that might be possible. He truly hoped it was.

The lions got to their feet, curious to see the feast that had arrived. The stone groaned as the keepers pushed it into place. Gubaru couldn't watch. He pressed his own seal hurriedly into the soft clay as was customary. He had to do everything correctly or the commissioners would ensure he received the same treatment as Daniel. He despised them for their selfish, wicked hearts. For personal gain, they would sacrifice the prosperity of all Babylon, casting away the gentlest, wisest man to ever advise the city. *Why had he ever appointed them? Why had he ever believed them an appropriate choice?* He pressed his noblemen's seals beneath his own, then hurled them to the ground in his anger and trod them in. He turned and hurried back to the palace, wiping tears from his face with the back of his hand as the sun disappeared behind Babylon's walls.

That afternoon, Gubaru had ordered his servants to bring him all the records of the law so that he could undo what he had done, before the appointed hour. He'd scoured them. He'd personally read every document he could lay his hands on, looking for the way in which he could pardon Daniel for breaking the statute of the law. *Surely he could do that? Surely it was within his power as ruler of Babylon to grant clemency when he saw fit?* His servants brought his food, but Gubaru didn't stop to eat it; he needed to find that one clause – one sentence – that stated his power to overrule a decision, revoke a law. The pile of discarded legal documents grew taller, the afternoon wore on and Gubaru began to feel sick. He read everything he could get his hands on with haste, rapidly scanning the words in his desperation. He had a hopeless sense that the task was impossible, and he snapped at anyone who spoke to him.

Late in the afternoon, the commissioners had entered the room and Gubaru had refused to look at them. He'd continued his search uninterrupted, ignoring their gloating presence, certain that he wouldn't be able to restrain himself to act responsibly if he saw the smug smiles on their hateful faces.

'Recognise, O King, that it is a law of the Medes and Persians that no injunction or statute which the king establishes may be changed.'

They tossed their document on the pile in front of Gubaru. He bit his tongue hard to prevent saying anything he'd regret – they'd probably find a way to have him publicly slaughtered for it – and ignored their stupid statute and them, concentrating only on holding himself together while the swept out of the room. Then he dropped his head into his hands and let the tears come.

'Did you not sign an injunction that any man who makes a petition to any god or man besides you, O King, for thirty days, is to be cast into the lions' den?'

The words haunted Gubaru's sleepless night. He muttered aloud the thoughts in his head. 'Yes. Yes, I did. I signed it. I brought this. It's my fault. I'm sorry. I'm so sorry. It's my fault.' He paced the room, thoughts of mauling and maiming, tearing and teeth and tragedy consuming him. *How could he have left Daniel there?* For that, he hated himself.

Why had he replied, 'The statement is true, according to the law of the Medes and Persians, which may not be revoked'? Why had he reminded them it was irrevocable? He'd given those scheming miscreants everything they'd needed – the power, the law, even the way to outwit him.

They were like children, running to their parent with tales of a sibling's misdemeanour, revelling in the report, delighting in the pain they were inflicting on their own flesh and blood. He could hear their mocking voices, see their eyes lighting up in anticipation as they spoke. 'Daniel, who is one of the exiles from Judah, pays no attention to you, O King, or to the injunction which you signed, but keeps making his petition three times a day.' People were so cruel, thought Gubaru. So unbelievably, inherently cruel.

Who cares? Gubaru had wanted to shout at them. Cyrus let the exiles go from Babylon and provided them everything they needed to go and worship Yahweh. Daniel stayed of his own volition to continue serving Babylon. Putting his own interests aside and working for the good of the city that held him captive – by choice! Why shouldn't he retain the prerogative to pray to Yahweh if he so chose? Surely he'd earned at least that? And what had happened to the tolerance and acceptance that Cyrus had bestowed? What had Babylon done with it?

But Gubaru knew the answer. He knew exactly what had happened to Daniel's right to pray. Because his own despicable hand had signed it away.

Chapter Fifty

I'm in Babylon's game reserve, taken captive, walled in and walking among lions. It occurs to me that it's an interesting metaphor for my life. I'm old now. My bones grow weary. I'm no longer the boy who ran to Jerusalem's olive grove, or the young man who survived the early days with Nebuchadrezzar by his quick wits and a large helping of Yahweh's guidance. I'm not even the man who watched him lose everything to truly understand his position in this world. I've seen Babylon's greatness soar to the heavens, and its influence spread like the tide, only to be undermined from within. And I've seen its impenetrable walls penetrated, the greatest work of its wit – outwitted.

I'm tired. I walked into this den of lions, not afraid as I should have been in the face of such threat, but heavy-hearted. I cry out to Yahweh for humanity, in all its depravity and with all its self-destructive behaviours. I long for people to listen to the lessons of history and learn from them, but watch with sadness as each new generation repeats the mistakes, over and over... Hurt, confusion – all the horrendous waste, unnecessary consequences of rebellion against Yahweh.

I sit down next to the head of a male lion and gaze at it in wonder. His head rests to one side on his front legs, the prominent claws a potent reminder of the power of this creature. Asleep, the features of his long face appear solemn, lent dignity by the semblance of responsibility and gentle thoughtfulness. Its mane forms a regal crown around its head. It's majestic. A tear trickles from my eye. I'm overwhelmed by the experience. Awed at this opportunity to get so close – gain such insight... In this moment, I understand for the first time what the kings of Babylon saw when they chose images of lions to adorn the length of the processional way, and for the walls of the throne room.

I sit alongside the king of beasts, surrounded by Yahweh's protection, and listen to what my God whispers to me.

'Daniel, you have walked alongside the lions of Babylon and I have kept you safe. You have been held captive inside its conceited walls and I have not allowed its influence to change your heart. You have honoured me in everything and because of this, I subdued the lions and tamed them so that you would not be harmed.'

With tears still in my eyes and trembling with awe and gratitude for Yahweh's presence with me, I reached out and stroked the lion's mane. In its sleep, it exhaled deeply. Peacefully.

Even though it had cast me to the lions to be devoured, I chose to love Babylon still.

Chapter Fifty-one

Babylon

As the sun rose over Babylon, the lion woke. It stretched its limbs and arched its back and pushed itself gracefully to its feet. The lion prowled. It sniffed at the morning air.

And then it pounced.

Propelling its weight with its hind legs, the lion reared up and fell on the human flesh that had been deposited in its enclosure. A scream punctured the calm. The lion was hungry. With its claws, sharp as a sword, it tore strips of skin and flesh, exposing red, raw insides. Blood, like spilled wine, poured into the dust. It stretched open its jaw, wide and strong. A flash of teeth. A deafening roar. The jaw snapped shut, clamping its keen teeth around the head of its meal and swinging it through the air. The body flew, limp, limbs trailing, blood spraying, depositing its entrails. It hit the ground hard. A broken empty carcass of a man.

The other lions were upon it in an instant. The stench of raw meat filled the air. Sounds of ripping, chewing, crushing echoed within the enclosure. A growl.

Gubaru looked away. The sight was unbearable. This practice was an abomination. He was seeing it in a new light. He threw his arms round Daniel and sobbed. Daniel held and comforted him.

The commissioners who had plotted this grotesque fate for Daniel would soon experience their own demise by the lions' terrifying destructive power. But first they would suffer a scene too painful to bear. They were forced to watch as their own children were sent one by one into the den. And then their wives.

To die.

To be dismembered.

Devoured.

Destroyed.

Chapter Fifty-two

I was born in Jerusalem in the reign of King Josiah. His legacy prepared me for everything I would face in Babylon. But in that city of decadence, Josiah's legacy became my own. By his example, I chose obedience to Yahweh over obedience to the powers of the world.

When Nebuchadrezzar wanted me to eat food offered first to Babylon's gods, I refused. When the commanders tricked Gubaru into creating his new law, I continued to pray to Yahweh. Time and again when it appeared that I would lose everything for my faith, I gained more than I could have imagined by staying true. I had been promoted multiple times to reach my current position of influence. My life had been spared more than once.

I was nearing the end of my days in Babylon in the reign of Gubaru. And I was glad. Yahweh granted me success and prosperity in those days. And what Nebuchadrezzar had begun to understand, Gubaru and Cyrus truly seemed to grasp and they declared it to the world. They sent a decree from the palace in Babylon to every people group, nation and language in the earth, sealed with the royal seal that guaranteed its authenticity:

May your peace abound! I make a decree that in all the dominion of my kingdom men are to fear and tremble before the God of Daniel;

For He is the living God and enduring forever,
And his kingdom is one which will not be destroyed,
And his dominion will be forever.
He delivers and rescues and performs signs and wonders
In heaven and on earth,
Who has also delivered Daniel from the power of the lions.

I chose Yahweh and showed that choice through my actions – actions which seemed totally incongruous in the city, but which were noticed, and which influenced and changed the culture. First in Babylon, and now beyond.

Note for the reader

The events depicted in *Babylon* are based on the stories recorded in Daniel 1–6 (together with episodes from Jeremiah). The author has woven these stories together with historical and archeological evidence of life in Babylon to help you explore the difficult questions that the Bible text raises. The author has used the spelling Nebuchadrezzar, an alternative spelling of Nebuchadnezzar.

Read the Bible passages about Daniel, Nebuchadnezzar and the other rulers of Babylon and reflect on what they tell you about God. What is God saying to you through these stories? If you have any questions, find a Christian you trust and chat through your ideas, thoughts and concerns.

What are Dark Chapters?

What is the Christian response to the vast array of horror books aimed at young people? Is it to condemn these titles and ban them from our shelves? Is it to ignore this trend and let our young people get on with reading them? At Scripture Union, we believe this presents a fantastic opportunity to help young people get into the pages of God's Word and wrestle with some of the difficult questions of faith.

The text does not sensationalise the horrific aspects of each story for entertainment's sake, and therefore trivialise what the story has to say. On the contrary, each retold account uses the more fantastic and gruesome episodes of each character's story to grip the reader and draw them into assessing why these events take place.

The reader is asked throughout the books to consider questions about the nature of God, how we should live as Christians, what value we place on things of this world – power, wealth, influence or popularity – and what God values.

The Oncoming Storm

Noah has been called by the Holy One, called to build an ark to escape the Holy One's judgement on the people of the earth. But Noah is the only person still faithful to the Holy One – who will believe that destruction is coming? They are too busy worshipping their own gods to listen to Noah – the Holy One will stand their faithlessness no longer. The storm is coming…

The Oncoming Storm

Andrew R Guyatt

£5.99
978 1 84427 619 6

Legion

A man rages on a hillside, driven mad by the voices in his head.

A man sits in a dungeon, plagued by doubt and fear.

Both are crushed by their demons. For one, freedom is only moments away, but for the other, it is only the end of his life that is near. Jesus is central to both their lives, but which one will live? And which one is about to face a terrible death?

Legion and the Dance of Death

Andrew Smith and Alex Taylor

£1.99
978 1 84427 623 3
£15 for a pack of 20
978 1 84427 629 5

Izevel, Queen of Darkness

Slowly, slowly, slowly, Izevel Princess of Tyre, works her influence over her new husband, Ahav, and his kingdom Israel. Leading them away from Adonai, she encourages the unspeakable practices of Baal worship. But despite her best efforts, the Lord and his prophets will not be disposed of so easily. Increasingly driven mad by her own lifestyle, Izevel races headlong towards her own grisly downfall.

Izevel, Queen of Darkness

Kate Chamberlayne

£5.99
978 1 84427 536 6

The Egyptian Nightmare

Pharaoh is ruler of all he surveys. His kingdom is prosperous and his monuments are being built at a fantastic rate by his Hebrew slaves. But suddenly, Moses and Aaron appear in his palace and demand the release of the God's people. As events spiral out of his control and God strikes his country with terrifying plagues, Pharaoh's desperate attempts to regain power only lead to his own destruction.

The Egyptian Nightmare

Hannah MacFarlane

£5.99
978 1 84427 535 9

The Sky will Fall

Shimsom thought back over all he had achieved for the Lord. He was one of God's judges, appointed by the Lord to guide his people and rid them of Philistine rule. But Shimsom's methods – a donkey's jawbone, pairs of foxes, a Philistine marriage – had led him here, tied to pillars in the Temple of Dagon. But if he was going to meet a gruesome end, then he would take everyone else with him…

The Sky Will Fall

Darren R Hill

£5.99
978 1 84427 537 3